To Hyla and Aster
Magic is real, and it always will be so long as you believe...

*"By the pricking of my thumbs,
Something wicked this way comes."*
William Shakespeare, Macbeth (4.1.44-45)

Contents

Prologue
Part I:
The Bird and the Worm..11
Part II:
Old Folktales 79
Part III:
The Bone Lady...99
Part IV:
The One Who Walks In Darkness...139

Prologue

August, 2017

Danny Fletcher was sitting on the living room floor flipping through his favorite Berenstain Bears tale when he heard a loud thump against the window. The suddenness of the noise startled him, but then, it didn't take much to get a six-year-old's imagination going…especially one as active as Danny's.

"Daddy," he called nervously. He sat upright, an unconscious tactic to make himself appear larger. "Wh…what was that?"

He stared at the window, his nerves on edge, and listened for a response from his daddy. He strained his hearing, squinted his eyes, and looked at the wall as he tried to concentrate.

Thump!

He jumped back and slid across the floor on his butt. "Daddy!" he called louder. "What was that noise?"

It was the same dull thump as before, as if someone were slapping the window with a glove or pillow over their hand. This time, it was followed by a light scratching against the glass.

"Wait a second, Rhonda," he heard his father say. The house was still and Danny could hear his parents arguing in the other room.

"This isn't something that can wait," Rhonda replied, her voice sharp and accusatory. "You *know* what that...that, thing can do. You *know* the damn consequences, Sam."

"Would you be quiet and stop acting like a scared little child?" Sam walked to the doorway leading to the living room and stuck his head through. "What do you need, buddy?"

Danny sat quietly, eyes glued to the window, his book clutched tightly in his hands. "Something just hit the window."

"Hit the window, huh? Is someone there?"

"What's wrong?" Rhonda asked, pushing her way past Sam.

"He said he heard a noise, Rhonda. I'll take a look. Jesus, let me handle this."

"No, I don't think anyone is there. It sounded *different* than a person," Danny replied.

Sam made his way toward the large window, shifting his eyes back and forth in search of the sound's source. The tree tops swayed in the wind and he noticed dark clouds covering the sky as they pushed over the mountains.

"Oh, I see. Looks like a storm's movin' in. It was probably just a branch or something blowing over, buddy." He turned to Danny and grinned. "Nothing to worry about." He started toward the kitchen when the same scratching noise that Danny had heard caught his attention.

Danny looked at him, curiosity beaming from his eyes. "You hear that? What is it, Daddy?"

Rhonda looked over at Sam, a combination of anger, fear, and anxiety filling her chest. She opened her mouth to speak, but before she could, he raised his hand. "I don't wanna hear it, Rhonda. That's *not* what this is." He squinted and looked to the window. "But there is something out there."

Head cocked to the side, Danny tip toed over to the glass, cautiously placing his hands on the sill. "I think it's coming from down there." Inch by inch, he moved his face closer to the window until his forehead pressed against the glass. "Daddy! It's a bird! I think it's hurt!"

Sam's face lost all color, as if his soul had suddenly fled his body leaving nothing but an empty vessel in its place. He tried to swallow, but it stuck in his throat causing him to choke. "A-a bird?" He loosened the collar on his shirt, unbuttoning the top button. "Wh-what k-kind of bird?"

"Sam," Rhonda said, her voice taking on a nervous tone.

Sam neared the window and his eyes widened as what lay beneath him on the other side of the glass came into his full view. "Oh, no," he said quietly, staggering backward. "I-it's a..." He hesitated a bit, unable to find the words. His hand clutched his chest and gibberish slurred from his mouth. "J-Jeschrist. I-i-it, c-c-canbe."

"What's wrong, Daddy?"

Sam closed his eyes and took in deep breath, releasing it slowly. He repeated this maneuver several more times until his heartbeat came under control. "I-it's a, a..." He didn't want to say what it was. He couldn't. The mere identity of the bird, once uttered, lay claim to the stories as being more than just that – more than *just stories*. He stared at it for a while trying to convince himself that it was something different, or that it was all just some sort of big coincidence. But deep down, he knew what was happening. There was no other bird like this, jet black with empty, hollow eyes. He scanned the body of the animal, his eyes falling on its chest, locking onto it like a castaway's eyes lock on to the first sight of a rescue ship. "I-it's got the mark, Rhonda." he whispered.

"Sam, you're scaring us," Rhonda said, so calmly that even Danny could tell it had been forced.

Sam swallowed hard and cleared his throat. "It's a crow, Rhonda. It's a fucking crow. And it has the mark." He smiled an odd sort of smile, one that gives the false impression of hope. His nervousness grew obvious to his family, his forefingers erratically rubbing his thumbs, the constant licking of his lips, his hands massaging the back of his neck, eyes jittering back and forth in his head.

"Why did you have to go there, Sam? Huh? Why did you ever have to go down into that godforsaken hollow? You know that place is forbidden. Nobody ever goes down in there!"

"I-I didn't mean to go over there, I swear. I-it just… it was *calling* me. It called me right to it, you know?"

"*It* didn't, Sam. *She* did." Rhonda ran into the bedroom, returning with a small black book. "Here," she said, shoving it into Sam's arms. "You took the damn thing, you can take it back."

In his hands was a small black leather-bound journal. He ran his finger across the cover. An inverted triangle embedded into the material, symbolic of what the book held. What should have been its apex extended beyond to form two curly lines below. In the center was an 'X', its lines originating from the triangles base. Below the shape was a 'V'.

Prologue

"That's the fucking Seal of Satan! The fucking *Seal of Satan*, Sam!"

At the window, Danny watched the bird struggle as he listened to his parents argue. Drop by drop, rain began to splat against the porch as black clouds took over the last remaining bit of daylight. The light was fading, but in the distance, he saw something. He squinted, unsure of what it was or if it was even real. *The sky looks like its...* He paused, mid-thought. *It...it is.*

"Something's happening," Danny shouted. "The sky, it looks like it's getting closer."

The screaming between his parents continued, his words unheard.

"Daddy? Mommy? The sky is coming to the house."

"It's just a story!" Sam yelled. "Sh-she was just an old woman."

"It's not just a story, Sam. It never was just a story! Gunrack Hollow is cursed!"

"Please," Danny cried, his voice reaching its highest peak. "It's coming! I-it's scaring me."

"Have you even seen inside of it? It's inked in *blood*! It's full of—"

"It can take all of our problems away!" Sam interrupted. "Th...they told me so."

"No, Sam. That's how she tricks you. That's how she gets you to cross the line."

"Please!" Danny yelled, and threw his Berenstain Bears book at them. "Stop screaming! The sky is falling!"

Their attention turned to their son, Sam and Rhonda ran to him and watched as he pointed toward the sky, his hand trembling violently.

"What's wrong, Danny? What's happening?" Rhonda clutched him in her arms and Sam rushed to the window to see what he was pointing at.

"My God…they're…here."

Crows sliced through the storm in droves. Hundreds of them pushing through the rain with minimal effort. They were coming for the house, wings flapping with a fierceness and determination unlike any Sam had ever witnessed.

"Take Danny to our room and lock the door."

"What is it, Sam?"

"Crows."

"Wha—"

"Just go!"

But it was too late. The crows bounced against every window until the force became too much for the glass to withstand. Within seconds, the birds filled every room. Danny screamed and Sam jumped on top of both him and Rhonda, covering them as best he could. The birds landed all over Sam and Rhonda, tearing at their hair and skin with massive, sharp beaks, ripping bits of hair and flesh from root and bone.

Still clutching the book under his arm, Sam grabbed a lamp from the end table and began swatting them out of the air. He took a blanket from the couch and tossed it to Rhonda. "Keep him safe!"

Sam stormed across the room swinging the lamp like a baseball bat and taking the crows out one by one, but just as he'd started to make a bit of headway, a single loud clap of thunder that seemed to shake the entire earth erupted from the heavens. He staggered back and dropped the lamp, the book not far behind. He thought about grabbing it, but the instinct for survival helped to override that of the books promises, so he covered himself instead, ready to protect his body. But there was no need. Just as the thunder clapped, the crows fell from the sky, covering every square inch of ground before him like a massive black sea of feathers.

He turned to his family. "Jesus, are you all okay?"

In a sudden jerk, Danny pushed his mother away with enough force to send her crashing to the ground and walked slowly to the middle of the room before he turned to face the window. He pointed toward something outside and began to make a strange mixture of grunts and high-pitched mumbling sounds.

Sam looked to Rhonda, then started toward Danny, cautious of his actions. "What is it, buddy?"

Danny turned to his family and smiled. His eyes rolled back in his head exposing nothing more than the whites, and he fell back to the floor, twitching and shaking violently.

"Danny! Sam, help him!"

As if gravity had suddenly lessened its strength on Danny alone, his body lifted from the floor, suspending in mid-air, a large and eerie smile resembling a badly molded Halloween mask still stretched across his face. He took in a deep breath and began to yell out in a shrill hiss. "Witch! Witch! Witch! Witch!"

Rhonda started screaming hysterically, grabbing at his feet with all her strength trying to pull him back down to the safety of her arms. "Do you see now, Sam? Do you see what you've done to your son?"

"Witch! Witch! Witch!" Danny screamed, pointing to something outside of the house.

Sam looked toward the door and saw that the rain had stopped. Not stopped as in it was no longer raining, but stopped in the sense that it was still. It had frozen in space, hovering motionless in the air.

What in the name of God is happening?

In the distance, a silhouette appeared near the end of their drive. Sam walked toward the doorway to get a better look. A wind filled his ears, one that sounded like voices whispering to him, and he realized that it was the same voices that had called him to take the book, tempted him to take it.

No, he thought. *Rhonda was right. It was all a trap. I-it was her the whole time.*

A vibrant streak of lightning filled the sky, its brightness temporarily blinding, and a second clap of thunder echoed with a force so powerful that it sent Sam and Rhonda slamming into the wall.

***

Sam was the first to wake. He raised up and scanned the room, his hands comforting his throbbing head. Rhonda was laying in the corner, still unconscious. He started for her but his muscles seemed to be locked, like his knees and ankles had somehow been filled with cement. To his side, he heard an unknown but at the same time unmistakable sound. It was a sort of a raspy whine. He turned to see and found himself staring at a shadowy cloud hovering over Danny's still suspended limp body. Within seconds the dark, vaporous mist began to take form. From the center of the black, smoky blob came what Sam could only imagine was supposed to be a head, followed by two

Prologue

longer globs that he quickly realized were meant to be its arms.

Unable to move, Sam watched as a combination of awe and fear fought for dominance deep within him. He'd never seen anything quite like it before, at least not in reality. He'd heard the stories all his life, but fantasy and old holler hoodoo was something he'd never held in high regard, especially as something with any *real* merit. He swallowed hard as the cloudy apparition continued to develop, swirling about in the air above his son like some sort of intelligent, sinister fog. In what looked to be the thing's head, three dark spots appeared – a mouth and two eyes, Sam deduced. Long, stringy fringes dangled from its top, reminding him of the hair of a worn and discarded baby doll, one forgotten by its once loving child-mother, and his brain finally made the connection.

It was a woman. It was the witch.

She floated just above Danny's face, crowding him in her presence. A long black segment resembling a tentacle slithered from what appeared to be her mouth. "How delicious," she hissed, glancing over to Sam. "His soul will serve me well. It's a strong one." In one motion, the witch opened her mouth and held it over Danny's. From his very core, something began to emerge, moving from his stomach to his throat and from his throat to his mouth, his insides twisting as whatever it was pushed upward.

Sam looked on, still unable to move as a coal black mass surrounded by a thin gray smoke exited his son and went into the witch, leaving his body a shriveled mess of stiff, dried skin that clung to bone like plastic wrapping.

"This will serve as the price you pay for crossing into *my* holler," the witch said.

"But...I didn't mean to. P-please," Sam pleaded, but a loud shriek from the fog rattled him, echoing in the air.

"You took something of mine, so now I return the favor." She floated over to the book, surrounding it in a thin mist. "One of many tricks, and one that *always* works so well."

Sam gasped, his heart dropped into his stomach as he was left to face the reality of what he'd done, what his actions had led to, and now there was no more book. It was never his, he thought, the witch had used it to have a way of coming into his life and stealing the one thing he loved most.

As quickly as the storm had begun, the black clouds drifted apart, evaporating into nothingness until sunlight filled the room. The witch vanished with them, obliterated by the daylight, and in a tired, depressed, and mournful state, Sam collapsed onto the floor.

Part I:

The Bird and the Worm

1

October, 2019

Anthony Fletcher took a deep breath and tossed a handful of old nails into an empty coffee can he'd placed on the floor. He wasn't really sure why they'd brought them along. He'd thought their use a little extreme for such a fragile subject. Too savage a method, maybe? Too primitive? But that didn't matter. Not really. He did what he was told, even if it seemed over the top. He looked back at Sam, his 'brother from another mother' they'd always joked, and studied his demeanor.

His eyes were narrowed, fists balled up and clenched tight against his sides.

The cool October wind whipped around the side of the cabin, rattling loose boards as a crisp Autumn chill pushed its way inside through the many cracks and crevices scattered along the walls.

"You sure you wanna do this?" Anthony grunted, his voice deep and strained. "Once you start, there's no goin' back."

Sam's head hung low, his face expressionless, locked in a dead stare straight ahead. It was as if every ounce of hatred he'd ever harbored for anyone or anything throughout his entire life had somehow, in this one small instance in time, surfaced to focus on a single object ahead of them in the darkness. He took in a deep breath, steadying himself. "Absofuckinlutely. Why the hell else would I be up here tonight? It's what we came for."

Anthony pressed his lips together and a sense of uncertainty filled his stomach, tightened around his chest. "Okay," he grumbled, shrugging his shoulders nervously. "I...I just wanted to...no, I *needed* to make sure." He took a tube of cement glue and a plastic sandwich bag filled with salt from a brown burlap sack that hung across his shoulder. "It's just that...well, what if, I don't know." He twisted the top off of the glue and poured it over the nails as he talked, careful to coat each one with the thick, sticky substance. "What if somebody finds out about this? You know we could go to jail, right?" He grabbed the salt and turned it upside down, spilling the entire bag onto the glue coated iron cores. "This would pull some *real* time, not just a night or two like we used to do for public intoxication. I mean, we're talking about *murder*, Sam. For fuck's sake, this is some real shit. I've been in some shitty situations before. Not like this, but not much better, either." His mind trailed off, the memory of a wet, dark space...his naked skin against a concrete floor...his mother on top of him... his father in the corner. He shook his head to drive the memory back down, then continued. "But you, Sam...just, shit can go south fast. Are you sure? *Really* sure?"

Sam's face held strong. His chest moved up and down with each forceful blow as his breathing increased, and Anthony knew he'd struck a nerve.

"Look, buddy, I'm not sayin' you can't handle it. Trust me, I know you miss him. I've got your back. I really do. Hell, you always had mine. But you need to be absolutely positive of what you're doin' up here before it's too late. Murder ain't somethin' to fuck around with. Especially when you ain't got not evidenc—"

The Bird and the Worm

"Murder?" Sam replied with a slight chuckle, his stare still locked into the darkest corner. "You really think it's murder, huh?"

Anthony's eyes shifted around the room, his eyebrows raising as if an obvious observance had gone unnoticed. "Well…yeah, Sam, I do. What else would you call it? Think about what you're accusing somebody of here. Them was just stor—"

"Justice," Sam replied, matter-of-factly. "Justice is what I call it. Besides, it's only murder if what you're plannin' on killing is human. Ain't nobody gives one shit if you squash a goddamn cockroach. How is this any different?"

Anthony was quiet. He closed his eyes, squeezing them tight, and wiped his face. "Look, think about what you're saying. It…it doesn't make any sense, man. All that crazy talk about magic and shit, you know that ain't real, right? Your daddy even said it back then! When somebody dies, they're just gone. Ain't but two places after this life, and that's Heaven and Hell. Bible even says so."

Sam's breathing grew choppy, his emotions beginning to surface.

"And I know the stories. I was around too, remember? I sat right there as your daddy told 'em. Everybody 'round here heard 'em as kids." He glanced to the corner. "Hell, your daddy was the only one who ever took the time to tell me any of 'em. He was the only real dad I had. I remember the exact one you're talkin' about. The souls, the book of spells to raise the dead, the commandin' of animals, all of it. But you can't still believe that stuff, Sam. It was all just made up stories to scare us. Just stories for camping trips and makin' us to be good.

They ain't no such book. That just can't happen." He chuckled, an attempt at easing the growing tension that filled the room. "You've gotta know as well as I do that there's no such thing as wi—"

Sam raised his hand and slammed his fist into the wall. "You don't *have* to believe me, Anthony! I never *asked* you to believe me, goddammit! I just asked if you'd help me! That's all!"

Anthony was speechless. Sam was right, and he knew it. One thing he'd learned as a kid from Sam's old man was that if you make a promise to somebody, no matter what it is, you keep it. A man's only as good as his word, after all.

"No. I-I guess that's right."

Sam walked over and stood in the middle of the room next to his friend. "Right. And to be honest with you, I don't care what you believe right now. You weren't there that night. You didn't se—" Sam bit his lower lip, swallowed hard as a lump formed in his throat as he remembered the crazed look in his son's eyes when he screamed that horrid word into the night. "You'll see soon enough. When my…my *son*, comes back to me and this thing reveals itself for what it truly is."

Anthony nodded and thought about Sam's situation. He knew that he was still grieving, and that was understandable. Losing a child is something you never really get over, or at least that's what he heard. And the circumstances dealt to his family afterwards: the way authorities had found the boy; the suicide of Sam's wife and Danny's mother, Rhonda; the year and a half of court mandated therapy and psychiatrist visits that led to Sam's diagnosis of acute psychosis brought on by extreme bouts of stress. Everything culminated in this moment, and Anthony was worried about him. Genuinely worried. But, a promise is a promise. And he *had* promised, though he was wishing to God now that he'd made up some excuse why he couldn't. He scratched his head and smirked. "Well, I guess you got me, man. I wasn't there, Sam, you're right on that one."

"You guess I got you?" Sam repeated, seeming offended. "What do you mean you *guess I got you*? You agreed to help me, didn't you?"

Anthony nodded. "Yeah, I did. I just wanted to make sure you understood what you was doin' ain't just actin' out of anger and hate, and...well..." He trailed off, catching his tongue before the words *mental disorder* slipped.

Sam snorted. "And? Go on, Anthony. Go on and say it. *And* my *mental* disease, right?"

"Sam, man, calm down. It's just that, you can't be doin' stuff like this just 'cause you're mad or 'cause you hate somebody."

"Oh, I'm mad, and I really hate that bitch. But it's more than that, Anthony. Much more. More than you'd ever understand. This...*thing*...story or not, has taken everything I had, and now it's time for me to take something back." He thought back to that dreaded night. The witch had spoken a similar line to him regarding Danny's soul and that goddamn little black spell book she'd used to gain entrance into his life. Now, it was his turn to make her suffer. He snorted hard, spitting a massive glob of mucous onto the floor beside them. "Now, how about you shut the fuck up before you get us killed too, huh?" He shifted his neck to one side, then to the other, popping it. "What we believe or don't believe, that don't matter no more. Trust me on that. I ain't gonna bring you into this on lies. What matters to me is findin' out how to get Danny back."

Anthony nodded again, sympathy in his eyes. "But, it's been nearly two years, Sam. Don't you think the times come to try and find some peace? I mean, you remember when my old man ran off and left me in that fucking place, right?" Memories flashed in his mind again…his mother's smooth skin, the stench of cheap cigarettes that carried on his father.

Sam was quiet. His muscles began to tighten as he fought the urge to scream, to cry. Danny had indeed died in front of him and Rhonda almost two years ago, but letting it go wasn't an option now. It never was. He'd heard the stories about raising the dead and how some folks could do it, and if it was actually based in any sort of fact at all, even a hint of it, he wanted his chance.

"I know you're still havin' a hard time with all of this," Anthony continued. "You know, I loved that boy, too. But…" He hesitated, choosing his next words carefully. "Well, you know what happened. The medical examiner said he—"

"That medical examiner didn't see what I saw, either. That fucking whore over there stole him from me, stole his soul! I watched it leave his body, Anthony, and there was nothing I could do to stop her! And it was my fault, all of it! All because of that goddamn book!" He pointed toward the corner, eyes fixed on it like a cat's eyes fix on a trapped mouse. "She has it, and it holds her secrets. If there's a way, I'm gonna get him back."

Anthony held his hands out in front of himself in a defensive posture. "Okay, Sam. Okay. But, just know that, well…nobody blames you. Weird shit just happens sometimes."

In the distance, a single noise cut into the air. The volume was low, but the pitch was high. It's crude sharpness, different than the quiet night surrounding them, was enough to draw both Sam and Anthony's attention.

"What the fuck was that?" Anthony said, startled. "That didn't sound like the person I remember bringing up here." His eyes were wide, mouth hanging open.

Sam smiled giving his friend an 'I told you so' look.

When Sam didn't respond, Anthony smacked his arm. "Was that a fucking bird? Did a bird get in here somehow?"

The sound came again, slightly louder this time. It seemed as though it were closer to them, but they both knew that was impossible.

Anthony looked out the window. The darkness seemed to stretch for forever, the thick canopy hiding any last vestiges of remaining sunlight that dared creep over the mountain tops and down into the valleys below.

Again, a high-pitched squawk pierced the quiet one room hunting cabin, only this time it came from a different direction. This one came from outside. This one carried with it an invisible but strongly felt forcefulness that could only be directed at them.

Anthony shifted his feet. "Did that sound like…it couldn't have been, right? That wasn't the same sound as —"

Sam stared into the darkness. He gritted his teeth, his fists clenched to his sides so tightly that his knuckles were white and bloodless. "It's the goddamn crows. That's her animal, just like the stories. Come on, it's almost time. If you ain't gonna help me, then get the fuck outta here now and I'll do it myself. It's 'bout to get messy."

Anthony nodded. "O-okay, Sam. Whatever you say. You're same as family to me, buddy. My brother from another mother…and father, I guess, technically. I got you." He pressed his lips together, the normally pink hue turning pale under pressure. "I told you I'd help, and that's what I aim to do." He looked toward the corner and sighed. "Even if it does sound crazy."

"It'll all be fine after tonight, and you'll see for yourself who's crazy. Plus, I'll have my boy back." He walked to the window and looked out at the sky as if waiting for something to happen, something he'd witnessed in the past.

Something not so good.

The crow called again, the only sound from the outside world. It was as if the forest had been emptied by some higher power or mystical force. No rustling in the leaves, no owls hooting, no whip-poor-wills chirping. But now, a solitary bird stood high at the podium and gave his speech to the world; an evil speech, directed specifically to Anthony and Sam.

In the corner, the same loud squawking noise cut through the darkness.

"This ain't right, man. Something feels fucked up about this."

Sam jerked his head around. "You bring the shotgun like I asked?" he said, trying to give the impression of firmness and focus. It was time to get down to business.

"Yeah, Sam. Yeah, I brought it. Just like you wanted."

"Good. And the lanterns?"

Anthony fumbled through the duffel bag on the floor and listened to the growing intensity of what couldn't be mistaken as anything else. The sounds of a crow, and it was coming from the corner of the room. "Y-yeah. Got them, too."

His mind a rock as he focused on the task he'd been planning meticulously, waiting nearly two years to complete; Sam's mind was blindingly clear. He'd read all the folklore he could get his hands on, talked to the old folks in almost every holler around that would give him the time of day, and he was ready. He shrugged his shoulders, rolled his neck. "Listen, Anthony, I know that everyone thinks I'm crazy."

Anthony said nothing, only listened.

"I wasn't really clear in what I said when I asked if you was free to help me today. But I think you've got the idea now. I know your childhood wasn't the best, and there's a chance that all that shit may come back up tonight. That *thing* over there in the corner, she knows about it, too. She knows about lots of things, things nobody else in the whole world knows but you. It ain't gonna be easy. So, this is your chance to leave, no questions asked."

"Sam," Anthony started, but was abruptly cut off by his friend.

"I've never lied to you, man, and you *know* that."

Anthony saw that the serious look was gone now, replaced by one of sorrow and anguish and pain. The ghosts of his best friend's past had finally caught up to him, the memories wrenching his heart.

"But if you stay, I can promise you one thing. I'll owe you my life for what we're about to do, and you ain't gonna believe what you'll see."

The room was silent for a long moment, even the strange and lonesome squawking from the corner had faded. Anthony studied about what Sam had said, thinking ahead at what they were about to do. As he contemplated every scenario that could play out, every last possible outcome, one thing kept bouncing back and forth in his head, coming back around each time like a boomerang – the thought that Sam had, in fact, never lied to him. Sam had always been there for him when they were children. They'd banded together in the face of bullies and pretty girls alike, and although he tried to forget his past, he knew Sam was the single reason that he was even still alive.

"Sam," he said, breaking the silence. "I *do* think it's crazy, and you would too if our roles was switched. But, I also know that, you're like a brother to me. You'd do the same for me and not even think twice. Just like all them years ago when you found me locked up down in that dark hole. I've already come this far. Already in too deep now. I made a promise to you and I'm here to see it through."

Sam nodded in acceptance. "Okay. Shit's 'bout to get *real* ugly."

"I'm a big boy. I can handle it."

"Hand me the shotgun, then. It's about to start."

Outside, the lone crow called once more, but this time there was an echo.

Echo? Sam thought. *That's no echo. They're gathering. Just like before.*

Another call split through the quiet. Then another, and another, until the cries of the vengeful birds seemed to

The Bird and the Worm

stretch for miles. Their army was nearing, growing into thousands as their mother called to them from the shadows.

Anthony looked to Sam for a sign of what to do next.

Sam slid a handful of shells into the shotgun filling it full, then pumped one into the chamber. "Are you ready to show these goddamn fucking birds who they're messin' with?"

Anthony grabbed the lantern and set it on the floor between them.

"Turn on the lamp so we can see the bitch," Sam said. "They're hers, and I want her to see what's about to happen to 'em. I wanna see fear in her ugly ass eyes. I want that fuckin' bitch to be afraid of me."

2

Anthony reached over and flipped the switch on the battery powered lantern. Immediately, a beam of light stretched out into the night and across the wooden floor. It was just bright enough to illuminate a small circle around them, revealing everything within its radius.

The light and everything caught in its glow was the last thing on Sam's mind, though. Something had happened to him the moment his friend had flipped the switch. It was the sound, that crisp *click* of the lantern's switch had struck him in a strange way, and for a moment, he was lost. Something about that simple little sound nagged at his subconscious, dragged him away to another time, another place. His mind was foggy, like he'd just woken up in the middle of an eerie mental mist. In reality, somewhere deep in his mind, he knew that he was standing inside of what used to be his father's hunting cabin deep in a holler in the woods of Appalachia. But in his mind's current state, his *percieved* reality, he was somewhere else altogether. The drastic change confused him. He couldn't help but wonder if he'd somehow fallen into another world or dimension, one that was from long, long ago; a world that he knew for certain was no more.

His eyes widened and his mind flooded with memories. He saw his old bedroom, felt the carpet between his toes, and a weak smile fell on his face. There was a voice. It was feminine, soft and sweet.

Rhonda? Is that you?

He looked around frantically, his eyes darting back and forth as he scanned his new surroundings.

A-am I...home?

He turned to find his ex-wife standing before him, as beautiful as she'd ever been. He reached for her, but something was off. She was in the same room only a few feet away from him, but she seemed too far for him to reach.

"Hey Sam. Did you have a good time hunting this morning?"

He heard her voice again, saw her lips move, but it was different...in a strange way. It was almost as if the sound was out of sync with her mouth, like a badly dubbed monster movie from his childhood.

Hunting? What's happening to me?

Anthony looked to him, saw his pupils dilated. "Sam? What's goin on, man?" He watched as Sam extended a hand reaching toward the darkness. "Is... everything, okay?"

"Rhonda?" Sam whispered.

"Uhm, Sam...Rhonda's not there, buddy. What, uh, what are you talking about?" Anthony peered into the corner himself, squinting hard as he tried to make sense of what, or who, Sam was talking to. "Seriously, man. You're starting to creep me out."

Sam couldn't hear him, though. All he could hear was the sweet sounds of his dead wife's voice. He watched as Rhonda rounded the foot of the bed, so close but still so impossibly far. She held something in her hands.

Sam studied it, tried to make out what she had, and it looked vaguely familiar to him. It was some kind of journal, maybe. No, it was a book. A small black book, with some sort of shape engraved on the cover. He tried to see exactly what the shape was, but all he knew is that it looked like something he'd encountered before, and then it hit him.

"I was hunting," he whispered. "It...it *called* to me. It's a trick."

He heard another voice. A juvenile, a young child – a *boy*. It came again, from the other room. Sam's breath stopped, held in anticipation of something he was at one time sure he would never hear again.

Danny? I-it can't be.

His eyes began to swell with warm, salty tears as adrenaline flooded his bloodstream.

Just like a bad dream, one you can never remember when you wake because the scenes change so drastically and randomly, the scene in front of Sam switched without warning. Rhonda was arguing with him now, and he was unsure why. "Danny?" he called, waving his arms around the room like a madman. "D-Danny, wh-where did you go?"

Anthony's heartbeat increased. An odd feeling, one of unsettling terror settled into his bones. "Sam...man, you need to snap out of whatever the fuck it is you're in, man."

Sam was confused. He saw Rhonda yelling at him, staring in his direction, and he could hear himself yelling back, but he knew that it wasn't him yelling back at her, at least not the present him. They were arguing about money. They'd always argued over money, ever since they'd married. *That's what the book said*, he remembered. *It told me that if I took it, it could fix all of my problems. All of our problems.*

He heard the young boy's voice again, and this time it was calling for *him*.

"D-Danny?" he said quietly, his voice quivering. "I-I'm coming, buddy."

Growing more concerned for his friend's mental stability, Anthony strained to see into the corner. He wanted to see something, anything to make what was happening seem normal, but there was simply nothing there to see. "Sam," he said, his voice breaking. "Th-there's nobody there." He turned to Sam and suddenly felt his own heart rise into his throat before quickly crashing into his stomach. Sam's eyes had changed to solid white. Anthony grabbed him and shook him lightly. "Sam? Sam, I need you to talk to me, man."

Sam turned toward the bedroom door of his old house and a loud thud bounced against the window. He heard Danny calling him again, just on the other side of the door. He reached for the knob and twisted, stepping through as the door opened. As his second foot passed over the threshold of the doorway, Sam was back in the cabin. Anthony stood in front of him, the room completely dark except for the one small ring of light cast from the lantern. Rhonda was gone, and so was Danny. He looked around wildly, searching for his lost son and dead wife. "Wh-where did they…where did they go?"

Anthony shook him again. "Sam, what happened to you? You looked like you were somewhere else. Y-you was talkin' to…to somebody that, well, that wasn't there. I-it was…Rhonda, and Danny. Your eyes, they clouded over like you were dead or somethin', and you just wouldn't stop fuckin' smilin'. It was like you'd seen a ghost."

Sam turned around, looking in every direction for his lost family, his hands outstretched the entire time as if he expected to somehow find and grasp onto them again, one final time and, perhaps, pull them back from the next life through some kind of mystical make-believe doorway.

"I, I saw them! They were right there!"

"You saw who, Sam?"

"Danny and Rhonda?"

Anthony's face was one or pity. It was a face Sam had learned to recognize well over the past two years. "I'm tellin' you, Sam, there was nobody there," Anthony said, trying to calm him. "Nobody."

"B-but it was so…" His hands found his face and wiped it repeatedly. He slapped his own cheek to make sure he was really there. "I saw them, Anthony. I *know* I did." His lips curled downward into a frown, tears slipped steadily from the corner of each eye.

A quiet chuckle started in the corner of the room, slowly increasing in volume until it creeped into each of the men's ears like a stowaway tick on a mange ridden mongrel.

The light emitted from the lantern was just bright enough to cast a weak beam around the darkness, but not into it. It allowed minimal visibility into the corner, at best, turning everything beyond its reach into nothing more than a cascade of grays that blended quietly into blacks; shadows that faded from one shade to the next before turning to pure pitch at its deepest point.

As if operating on some unseen dictator's command, Sam and Anthony watched into the blackness. They didn't have to see it to know what made the noise.

They already knew. Hell, they'd put it there only hours before.

Sam stood motionless, attempting to regain his wit from the strange jump back in time. His mouth hung open, his breathing rapid and shallow. "I-it was her," he said, and pointed to the corner. "She did it. She made me see them. It was a fuckin' trick." He took a deep breath, gathering his emotions. "I told you, Anthony. I told you what she could do."

Another chuckle from the corner, this one followed by a rough rubbing sound, like wooden chair legs trying to scoot across an old wooden floor.

"Sam, what the fuck is going on?" Anthony said. "Do you hear her? She's fuckin' laughin'. How could she be laughin'? She's been over there for hours."

Without hesitation, Sam stepped forward, away from Anthony. "She's laughin' because she's enjoyin' it," he said with uncomfortable authority. "I've been tryin' to tell you, she's not what you think." He turned toward the noise. "Are you, *witch*?"

The laughter gained volume.

"What? You think that's funny, *witch*?" he yelled.

A high-pitched scream reminiscent of the old Irish banshee folktales swarmed from the shadows, the sound sending gooseflesh up Anthony's arms and onto his neck. With a sense of 'what on earth have I gotten myself into' shuttering through his bones, he turned to Sam. "Whhhaaaat the fuuuuck was that?"

3

"Get the light. Bring it closer." Sam took a step toward the darkness, his foot coming to rest at the edge of where the shadows swallowed the light and left their contents to the unknown.

Bewilderment struck Anthony as he unknowingly shook his head. *That laugh*, he thought, *that fucking laugh. It isn't right.*

He stared into the blackness, eyes squinted as if concentrating, his imagination conjuring thoughts of what may be lying just beyond the dull, piss-yellow beam.

"Anthony," Sam yelled. "The light! Bring it here!"

"O-oh," Anthony stuttered, jerking himself from his imagination and back into the moment. He tried to react quickly, but the jerkiness and uneven nature of his movements showed his growing level of anxiety. "Sure. Sorry, man." He picked up the lantern but was hesitant to move forward. He knew that once he did, the corner would be lit and its contents no longer allowed to hide. The woman they'd taken earlier in the evening would be visible to them, and that thought made him sick. It made his stomach feel as though someone were churning it in a giant pot with an equally large wooden spoon.

What they'd done to this point wasn't what set him on edge. He'd beaten drunks at bars worse than they'd treated the old woman in the corner, to this point at least. But there was something about this particular situation. Something about how the squawking noises seemed to be coming from her at first, something about how she just kept laughing, about how she just wouldn't stop and how she actually seemed to be enjoying being held against her will that made the hairs on his neck stand erect. Though he didn't want to admit it, the thing that *really* scared him most was the thought that maybe Sam had been right all along. What would he do if the person in that corner wasn't actually the woman they'd taken? What if she'd changed somehow? Her laugh *did* sound different than what he'd imagined it should've, and those godawful bird noises were nothing like what he'd expected an old woman should be able to do with her voice under such a high pressure, high stakes situation.

As he stepped forward, the lantern swayed on its handle causing the light to rock back and forth. In doing so it swung its gift of illumination, first to their front, then to their back. On each swing forward, two small squared wooden posts could be seen – the two front legs of an old chair – and each had what looked like a human foot sitting next to it. Anthony stared for a moment, his concentration fully locked.

The feet were tapping. Bouncing up and down in repeating methodical way. Not in a way that begged for freedom or reprieve like any normal person should be acting, given the current scenario. They were actually fucking *tapping*. The balls of each foot bounced up and down, tapping on the floor like a happy listener taps out the drumline to their favorite song.

Th…there's no fucking way this is real. Absolutely no fucking way.

"Come on, Anthony. Just a couple more steps. Don't be afraid of her. That's what she wants. She can only hurt you if you let her, if you allow her access inside your head."

A laugh came from the darkness. It was barely loud enough to be heard.

Slowly, Anthony lifted his right leg and placed it on the ground to his front. Then his left repeated the motion, forcing the light fully into the darkness as he went forward. It was enough to eliminate the last holds of gloom that seemed hellbent on clinging to the space.

Anthony gasped, his body staggering backward as he stared at the woman in a state of shock. His eyes sprang open wide, his face turned white. "Who the fuck is that, Sam? Th-that's not…that's just not *her*."

In an old wooden chair sitting in front of them was an elderly woman. Her limbs had been strapped to the ancient rotting frame with strands of rusted barbed wire. Her hair, long and stringy and gray, draped over her face in thin, messy clumps reminding them of some monster straight out the classic eighty's zombie movies. Her body appeared to be weak and emaciated, her bones pushing out against a grayish toned skin that looked like it didn't even belong on her. It was almost as if she wore a costume, one made of some flesh-like material, stretched tightly around her miniscule frame by some master designer.

"I told you, didn't I, Anthony? I told you you'd see."

"But, I-I don't understand. Wh-where did…where did she go? The woman we brought up here, what happened to her?"

The old woman looked up at him and smiled. Her eyes were sunk deep into their sockets, casting shadows over her face like the steepest mountains cast shadows over their most narrowed valleys. Her yellow stained teeth reflected the weak light of the lantern revealing numerous spots of blackened decay and rot.

Anthony winced. He exhaled a tired and broken breath, shivering like a nervous school girl asking her first date to prom. Confusion took him in its hold, squeezed his feeble, broken mind into submission, and his entire reality began to come unhinged. He remembered capturing a woman, yes. He remembered thinking that, at the time, Sam just may be a little nuts for blaming someone, especially her, for what'd happened to Danny. But now he wasn't so sure. Now, he was beginning to have his first doubt.

Where did she come from? It has to be a trick of the light…something. Or maybe I just didn't pay enough attention earlier in the evenin'. Yeah…that's it. Has to be.

This was different, though, and deep down inside of himself he knew it. Something had happened. Someone had pulled the old switch-a-roo on them when they weren't looking. The woman before him was not the same healthy, muscular woman they'd taken. *That* woman had been larger, she'd had weight on her bones. Her hair had been thick and golden. But this…this *thing* that was in front of them now, it was different.

"It was a trick," Sam offered. "That's what they do, what they're good at…this kind of witch. I've asked everyone around about 'em. They say they ain't many of 'em left out there, not like here, but there's a few. It took a little doin' for me to find her, but I did."

"This is crasy. I…just don't understand," Anthony responded.

"This is her. The *real* her. It's the same physical being, but this is her true form. I told you it wasn't what you thought." Sam slapped Anthony's back, breaking his attention. He looked at him, focused, serious. "Now, remember what I said before we came up here. Whatever you do, Anthony, you can't listen to her. Remember the stories? They get into your head. She's gonna…know things, put things in your mind. She's gonna say things to you that'll make you think bad thoughts, bring out your worst fears. They say it'll be like you're not here, or even that you're not you. And that's not just what I've heard. I don't know how to explain it, but that's what happened to me just a few minutes ago. I was here, but I wasn't. I blinked, and I was…well, I was just somewhere else."

Anthony shook his head slowly. "Th-this just can't be happening," he whispered. "They were just stories, Sam. Just *stories*."

The old woman chuckled. "That's right. They were and are *just stories*. It's not happening. In fact, you're both sitting around in your cozy little homes right now, cocks in each other's hands, afraid to admit that you're nothing more than a couple of *fags*."

"Where is the fucking book?" Sam yelled.

The old woman burst out in a fit of laughter. "The book? What…book? Surely you're not talking about that little black thing that got you into this mess in the first place?"

"I've got you now, and you're gonna tell us."

"Is that right?" she said, still laughing. "You have me? Are you sure it's not the other way around?"

"What is she talkin' about?" Anthony said, confused. "What's she mean?"

"Why, I let you think you had the same book you speak of now once before, and look what happened. What makes you think I didn't let you have me this time? I *hear* things, you know."

For a brief moment, the thought tried to take root in Sam's head. She had been easy to find, there was no doubt about that. She was practically out in the open. Sure, she *looked* different, but that's what he thought it would be.

No. I've made a mista...no. She wants me to think this.

He shook his head, fighting away the thoughts and getting back to business. "Tell me where it is or so help me God—"

"God?" she interrupted. "Really?" She slung her head up to face the boys. "You're *really* going to bring *Him* into this?" She looked to the sky, a large smile on her face. "Tell me, Sam, Samuel, or was it...*Sammy*, that your dear old daddy called you, hmm?"

Sam swallowed hard. He knew her games well.

"Oh, it doesn't matter, really. Both *God* and your father will be about the same help to you now."

"Shut your mouth, witch!"

"Never could stand to hear the *truth*, could you? You know it, neither of them helped you then, did they? Your precious *God* just let it all happen. Let your poor little son be taken from you, his eternal soul stripped from his body. It reminded me of gutting a fish. Isn't that what *God* is supposed to protect, souls of the innocent?"

"Shut your mouth!"

"I guess you can't really blame daddy, though. He's been dead since he crossed me years ago." She paused and looked around the cabin. "I do believe that it was right here where he drew his last breath, if I'm not mistaken. Yes! I ripped his heart from his chest in this very spot, to be exact."

Anthony took an uneasy step back. "Wh-what is she talking about, Sam? I thought your dad died in a hunting accident?"

"Oh, that's right. He did die in a hunting accident. He was hunting for the same thing that's going to kill you, wasn't he, *Sammy*? You know, the thing that…took your little *bastard* son from you!"

Sam began to quiver, thoughts of his dead son flooding his mind. He saw it happening again. Danny in front of him, levitating in mid-air. His body shaking, that one unforgettable word being screamed as he shriveled into nothing more than a dried, mummified corpse.

Anthony watched in amazement. "This is fucking crazy, Sam. This is getting too fucking nuts."

"Aww, poor little baby," the woman said, looking into his eyes.

As their vision locked, Anthony couldn't help but notice a lack of distinction between iris and pupil. It was as her entire eye had filled with one solid color; deep and black and glassy like obsidian.

She winked at him. "What's the matter, hmm? Little baby isn't afraid of a defenseless, old woman, is he? Or do I remind you too much of your *mommy*?" She jerked against her restraints forcing the chair up on two legs. "Let me loose, and I'll treat you just like she used to. I'll suck your little prick while dear ol' daddy watches and fondles his own, and when I'm done I'll throw you back down into that dark hole in the earth and leave you there to rot!"

Anthony jumped, turned his face from her to break eye contact. He saw a dark room in his mind, one he couldn't escape. He saw his mother there, her and his father…throwing him away. "Th-this ain't real," he whispered. "It can't be."

"Look at me, boy!" she commanded, her voice loud and sharp. "Look at me, or I'll rip your goddamn eyelids from your face and force you to watch me eat them like little slices of ham while I disembowel your chicken-shit friend!"

"The hell you will," Sam screamed, ramming the butt of the shotgun into her face as hard as he could manage. "I've had enough of this."

Her head snapped back, then fell to the front. She jerked about, her arms twitching erratically. A strange puffing noise started from her mouth and Anthony thought she was coughing, but as she raised her head again, he saw that it was laughter. Her lip had split all the way through from the impact, blood flowing freely from the exposed blood vessels of the wound, and she was still *laughing*.

Anthony became dizzy, staggering backward and then forward again before finally regaining his footing.

"Listen," Sam said to her. "Here's how it's gonna go. You're gonna listen first, and if you don't, I'll slice thin slits in your face and peel them off one piece at a time just to hear you scream. Do you understand?"

She writhed around wildly, a caged animal fighting for freedom. Low groans and grunts started in her stomach before creeping up into her chest like thick chunks of vomit, finally exploding from her mouth as her upper body rolled in the chair like a heroin addict going through withdrawals.

"You're going to tell me where the book is so I can bring my son back, or we're gonna take you apart piece by piece and feed you to those godforsaken fucking crows."

She stopped suddenly, her body becoming completely motionless.

"I-is she dead?" Anthony asked.

Outside, a crow cawed, followed by another, then another, until the relentless mocking made it impossible for them to hear anything else.

"Stop!"

"What the fuck is happening out there?" Anthony asked. "It sounds like there are hundreds of those…those… things."

The witch threw her head back and laughed. "My babies would never disrespect me like that. It's you who they'll feed on, you sorry sacks of shit. You're the ones who are about to be dismembered, and I'll make certain that it's a slow and agonizing process." She licked her lips, her tongue long and thin extending past the tip of her crooked nose. "And I'll enjoy sharing your raw flesh with each and every one of my little *devils*, just like I enjoyed swiping Danny's precious little soul."

Sam leaned over, his face mere inches from hers, and spit on her cheek. "Or maybe we'll just set you on fire and watch you fucking burn. You see, *witch*, I've heard the stories. I've done my research. I'm ready for you this time. I know how to hurt you." He looked to Anthony. "Let's see how she likes the hammer."

"Oh, no. N-not a hammer!" she mocked, grinning from ear to ear. "I've only been alive for nine-hundred years. I've never had a hammer used on me before. You've found my weakness! Please, no!"

The Bird and the Worm

Anthony reached into the sack and took out a small carpenter's hammer. He grabbed a few nails from the coffee can and handed them to Sam. He couldn't be sure of what was about to happen, but he had a decent guess. He watched as the woman laughed and smiled, bobbing her head as if she were having fun, and for a moment, he couldn't help but wonder if that was the case.

"Oh, look at that," she said, watching Anthony with interest. One eyebrow raised, mouth slightly open, she stared at him with the attention a heart surgeon pays his most critical patient.

Sam made a point not to look in her direction, but the never-ending verbal abuse made it nearly impossible to ignore her.

She saw Anthony's face. His mouth closed tightly, his brow arched downward. "Hey, you!" she yelled to him. "Yeah, I'm talking to you. You're being rude, don't you think? You know it's not polite to ignore an old woman. Why, what do you think your *mother* would say, hmm?"

Anthony shifted position, bounced from one foot to the other. His right hand found the back of his neck and started to massage it before sliding around to stroke his chin.

"Yessss, that's it. That's your happy place, isn't it? You always were a *momma's boy*, weren't you, Anthony?"

"You don't know anything," he said in a low voice. "You don't know anything at all about my life."

She grinned. "Is that so? I know more than you know yourself, stupid boy! I know that your sweet old momma had a special kind of love for her little baby boy. A *real* special kind."

He started pacing back and forth, the memories flooding back. He was just a little boy. It wasn't like he wanted it. He was too young to know the difference, to know right from wrong. He'd trusted her, trusted her to protect him. Isn't that what parents are supposed to do, protect their children?

His eyes started to burn. He could feel the tears welling up inside, trying to flow, but he bit his lip to force them back.

"Anthony," Sam said to him. "I told you she'd know things. You can't listen to her."

"This woman's crazy, Sam. I don't know who or what she is, or if you were right or wrong, but she's fucking psycho. How could she know this stuff?"

"You're just jealous that Mommy's not here to lick your little prick right now, aren't yo—"

Sam lunged at her, his fingers wrapping around her throat, a firm and steady pressure applied to her windpipe as he clenched it tightly. "Shut your goddamn mouth you fucking witch." He looked down at her as she began to gurgle, increasing the pressure against her esophagus little by little, an action that forced a stream of saliva from her mouth and down her chin as she choked for what little air he allowed her. "Now, let's try this one more time, how 'bout it?" He turned the hammer around showing her the clawed end used to remove nails from old boards. Forcing her head to the side, he pressed the claw into her cheek, pushing against it with a steady and firm pressure. "I'll tear your goddamn innards out of your body with my bare hands and leave them right here on this floor to rot, along with your black heart, you worthless piece of fuckin' shit. You hear me?" He pushed the claw of the hammer into her face with immense force until a tiny trickle of blood appeared, slipping down her cheek.

The crows called outside again, as if responding to Sam's threats.

The woman grinned, the split in her lip flapping as she moved her jaw to speak. "Th-re c-com-ing," she managed with a chuckle. "Th-thrcomng fryo."

Sam squeezed tighter, his fingernails sinking into her old, gray, wrinkled flesh. The constriction of her airway forced her eyes to bulge as she fought for precious oxygen. "That's right, *bitch*. Not so tough now, are you? Why don't you just tell us what we need to know and we can end all of this, how's that sound?"

She fought against his grip, but her bound limbs were no use in helping her. She struggled violently as she tried to pull free from the hold Sam had on her throat.

"The book, where is it?"

"S-Sam…she can't tell you if she's dead," Anthony said.

Still squeezing her neck, Sam slowly pulled the hammer away from her face and shoved her hard, releasing his grip at the last second. The force sent the chair back up on two legs. "That's not a problem. We can't kill her. Not like this anyway." He slapped her face, an action that sent a triumphant feeling from somewhere deep down inside of him. "Real satanic half breed devil whores like here have to be killed in a special way. Can't just shoot 'em or cut their throats. They're different than us."

She gasped repeatedly as she regained breath, each attempt nothing more than a wheezing gurgle. After a few long, deep breaths mixed with sinister laughter, the witch started to mumbled.

Anthony grabbed Sam's wrist, turning him around. "Wait a minute. What did you just say? Did you really just say that she can't die?"

"Yeah. That's right. Not like this, anyway. I mean, she *can* die, but not like you and me. Don't you remember? Dad used to tell us these stories all the time." He looked at the woman and took in a deep breath. "To kill a witch, you gotta burn her alive. Otherwise, she has to be killed by a stronger witch, or by her keeper. In this case—"

Anthony dropped his head slightly, his voice a mere whisper. "The…one who walks in darkness."

"Yeah. That's right. But I don't plan on meeting either of them. Once we get what we came for, we'll be able to do everything we need to do ourselves. You'll see."

"Ha!" The old woman shrieked, the humor in her voice obvious. "You honestly believe that I was stupid enough get captured by some halfwit like yourself? Someone with nothing more than revenge on their mind? Sammy…I thought you were smarter than this. Especially after what happened between you and I just a short time ago. What, it's only been two years, hasn't it? Surely you didn't expect to come into *my* holler and take something that belongs to me with the help of some pathetic little mamma's boy who can't even decide if he has a pussy or a dick to play with, did you?"

The thought occurred to him again. It had been easier than he'd imagined it should. All the old timers had told him that witches who don't wanna be found stay lost… they stay just the tales of old stories. It was almost like she'd wanted to be found.

No. We found her. There's no way she could've known that we were coming. But, why was it so easy?

The Bird and the Worm

Without warning, Sam spun around and slammed the hammer down on the witch's bare hand, the dull thud releasing a painful crunch into the night.

Her scream carried throughout the cabin like a siren, loud and sharp and unable to ignore, before descending into a series of guttural moans and raspy whines. A strange quiet fell over the cabin, a quiet that you feel as well as hear. The only sounds were those of the witch's deep, heavy breathing as she recovered from the trauma of the hammer's strike.

Anthony stared at Sam, speechless. Adrenaline pumped through his veins and he was visibly shaking as he tried to compose himself.

Suddenly, the woman's head whipped to an upright position, her eyes rolled back in her head. In a tone deeper than any she'd previously shown, one that seemed to be coming from someone else, she began to growl, moaning from the pit of her stomach. "Yoooouuuurrrrreeee mmaaaaaakkkkkiiiiinnnnggggg b-ig miiiiiissssssstttttttaaaaaakkkkke."

"I'm not leaving here until you tell me where that goddamn book is and how to use it to get my son back you fucking whore of Satan!" He reared back and slapped her again. "Tell us, now!"

Anthony's mouth hung open, jaw flapping like an open shutter in a summer storm. He'd never seen his best friend act like this before. He'd never known Sam was capable of such brutal and horrendous behavior. He shook his head in disbelief. "Something's wrong with her, Sam. Something's not right. M-maybe you should give it a rest, I don't know. Maybe we should—"

The old woman jerked upright, her back stiff and erect. "That was too easy, boy. See what I mean? Already having doubts, and you haven't even done anything to me yet. How do you expect to get anywhere with…" she glanced to Anthony, "*this*? His pussy must be aching for his poor dead mommy's fingers. Wah, wah, wah!"

In an instant, Sam placed the tip of the salt covered nail against her skin and dropped the head of the hammer on it. It penetrated with ease, driving through flesh and bone and into the chair's handle.

"Fuck!" She screamed with a force that rattled the glass in each window of the structure. She inhaled broken breath, like a small toddler pouting after being spanked for the first time. "I'm just an old woman! Why would you do this to me?"

"Shut up!" Sam protested. "You're no woman. You're a fucking witch! Now tell me, how do I get Danny back?"

The old woman looked into his eyes, still huffing erratically. Slowly, the edges of her mouth curled upward. Her voice dropped in tone, the sinister hiss replaced by a sweet, seductive sound. "Danny? Is that, *really* why you came to me, Sammy?" She twisted her arm around in the restraints until her hand lay palm up, blood dripping to the floor as the barbed wire ripped into her flesh. She motioned for him to come closer with her finger. The tips of the barbed wire dug deeper into the meat of her wrist until the drips of blood turned into a steady flow. "I've known you and your family for a very long while. Your father especially. You are a lot like him, you know? You're strong, masculine. You're a *real* man, Sammy." Her tongue slipped from between her lips, flicking up and down slowly.

Sam blinked, squeezed his eyes tight. Something was happening. He became dizzy. His focus was on the eyes of the witch now, but his mind began to wander. He could hear nothing, as if his eardrums had painlessly ruptured and left him deaf to the world. His eyes wide, he tried to look away from her, but the connection between his brain and his muscles had ruptured.

"That's right," she said, almost whispering. "Why don't you just let go of *Danny*? That's not why you came to me, is it? That's not the *real* reason." She thrust her hips back and forth, grinding smoothly against the chair. "I know exactly what you, *really* want. Why, you're so much like your father that it's pathetic, but in a cute way." She continued to motion with her finger for him to come closer. "And I can give it to you, right now, if you like."

"Sam?" Anthony said, watching his friend turn into a seemingly helpless zombie. "Sam...come on man. This ain't funny."

Sam took a step toward her, then another. He could feel himself trying to fight it, but the urge to go to her was too strong. In the chair now, he didn't see the small, wrinkly figure with stringy gray hair and cracked gray skin. Instead, he saw a beautiful woman with flowing auburn hair, her legs spread wide as she begged him to come for her. Reluctantly, he took another step, his thighs quivering with uncertainty.

"Rh...Rhonda?" he whispered.

"That's it, Sam. Why don't you come over here and let me give you what you *really* want? It's been so, so long, hasn't it? Too long, in fact."

He felt his lips move, a slight grin forming. Almost within arm's length of her, he tried to finish the distance, but he couldn't move. He wanted it now, more than anything, to be connected with his gorgeous wife again, and she was right there in front of him. The world had disappeared, nothing existed anymore but his beautiful wife. "Oh, Rhonda. I'm right he—"

He felt something hard slam against his face, the force sending him to the floor, and his senses came rushing back to him.

The stench of rotten flesh filled his nostrils. He looked up and the beauty in the chair had vanished; replaced, once again, by the hideous figure he'd come accustomed to only moments before. His face burned with pain, his head throbbing with immense pressure. He placed his hand on it for comfort and saw Anthony standing above him.

"Sam, are you okay?"

Still in a daze, he shook his head. "D-did you just hit me?"

Anthony looked over at the witch, who was cackling louder than ever, thrashing about in the chair. "What happened to you?"

Sam looked at her and winced. "I-I was... somewhere else for a minute. That's all. Don't listen to her, Anthony. Whatever you do." He grabbed another salty nail from the can and walked over to her. He struck her chest with the hammer, then drove the nail into her other hand.

"Fuck you," she screamed. "I'll see to it that you both suffer for this! He will want you for himself, now. You've interfered enough!"

The Bird and the Worm

"That's for what you just did, bitch. Now, this is your last chance. Tell me how to get Danny back! I know you can do it, they say the book has spells for it. Now tell me!"

"Danny, Danny, Danny," she whispered. "Poor little Danny boy. Is that all you can think about?" Her eyes drifted back and forth as she looked to each side, her voice bouncing from high to low, masculine to feminine, and every pitch in between. "You want your precious little Danny back so bad, don't you? Such a sweet little boy he was. I remember him well. Young. Innocent. I often wonder what makes you think that an old woman like me would even want someone like that." She paused, licked her lips, and cackled. "Perhaps he was a special gift. Did you ever think of that? He was one of a kind, wasn't he? Yes, he would make a fine gift."

Sam froze. The thought had never occurred to him. She'd taken his soul, sure. But what if she'd used it as a gift to her keeper? Given it to the one who walks in darkness?

"Now I've got you thinking. You wonder where he is, hmm? You struggle with *why* he was taken from you? Well, the way I see it is, it's just too bad he had such selfish, greedy parents. Why, if that weren't the case, he'd probably still be with you, don't you think? You wouldn't be here right now wondering if I traded him away." She let out another deafening laugh. "

Sam's muscles tightened, his entire body grew rigid. He took a deep breath and bit his lip. "I've about had all I'm going to take—"

"Really? You won't do a fucking thing. You're too *weak*. Why do you think Rhonda left you? Why do you think they found her in a cheap hotel room with a gun in her mouth and half of her fucking head blown off?"

He took a clump of her hair in his hand and yanked it. "Keep their names out of your mouth. *You* did that to us! You took my Danny, and you pushed Rhonda away from me!"

"Sam," Anthony said. "Calm down, man. Like you told me, you can't listen to her. That's how she works, remember? She's gonna say things she knows will get to you."

"You fucking cunt!" she yelled. "I'm going to eat your fucking heart from your chest as you beg me to make your pain go away." She looked at Anthony, a dead focus on him now. Her long lizard-like tongue slipped from her lips, gently caressing each one seductively. "And I see you finally grew some balls, hmm? Imagine that. You *can* speak after all?" Her voice was softer again, sweeter, almost motherly. She blinked slowly and, for a moment, Anthony thought he saw her eyelashes grow longer. She continued to rim her lips with her tongue. "I'll tell you what. You're not a bad looking specimen of a man yourself, *Anthony*. Why don't you come over here and let me suck on your cock like mommy used to, and you can ask me about Danny as you're about to cum, hmm?" She let out a loud burst of laughter and thrust her hips forward.

Sam grimaced and yanked her head back using her hair. The chair fell backward and he released his hold, watching it slam to the floor. He smiled and looked into her eyes. "Give me the salt, Anthony."

The look on her face changed from one of pleasure to one of worry, and from one of worry to one of enjoyment, all in the span of a second.

Sam stomped her stomach and as she exhaled, he clutched her jaw in his hand, forcing her mouth open. He opened the canister of salt and started dumping it into her mouth.

Her eyes widened and she began to wail as a loud sizzling came from inside of her. Smoke began to rise from her face as she screamed in agony, bucking and thrashing against her restraints like a rabid beast.

"I-is it actually burning her?" Anthony said.

Sam poured nearly half of the canister into her mouth until it spilled over and onto her face. She choked and flung her head from side to side, spitting the foreign substance at them with such force that it stung his cheeks when it hit. Inhuman sounds escaped from her body, filling the air with a sudden feeling of absolute dread.

Sam took hold of her hair again and used it to pull her upright, sitting the chair back on its four legs. The woman gagged and slung her head, trying to clear the offending salt from her airways. With each splotch of saliva that hit the ground, Anthony noticed a red tinge to it. He looked at the woman's face and all along her cheeks were red, bloodied holes. They were scattered across her skin from jaw to eye like splatters of red paint flicked from a brush against a gray leather canvas. Holes adorned her face, a mosaic of crimson stained pits.

"I-it ate her fucking skin, Sam. Tell me I'm not crazy. T-tell me I'm not losing it and that that fucking salt ate that fucking woman's face?"

"I told you you'd see." Sam said, grinning. "They don't like salt."

4

The crows called outside. Their cries seemed to stretch for miles in the apparent absence of any other lifeform beyond the four cabin walls. From the sounds of it, they were on top of the cabin now, just beyond the safety of the aged structure. The volume of their pleas suggested their numbers were high, and it was only a matter of time now.

The old woman chuckled quietly as she spit the remaining salt particles from her burning mouth. Her chuckles turned into a laugh, then grew into an all-out cackle.

The way it was all playing out reminded Sam of a saying he'd always heard his father say. There were many variations of the same phrase, all involving two animals, one the predator, the other the prey. "It's a classic case of the bird and the worm, Sam," his father would always say. "You always wanna be the bird…never the worm". He'd never known what it meant as a child, but right now he was getting it loud and clear, and as the crows' numbers continued to mount outside, he was feeling an awful lot like a worm.

Anthony paced back and forth, nervously. "She's absolutely crazy, Sam. That's the only fuckin' explanation for any of this. This whole fuckin' thing is just *nuts*! I mean, look at her. Her fuckin' skin was melting off because you poured table salt on her for Christ's sake…and she's laughing like she enjoys it!"

"Physical pain," the woman started, "is something that lies very close to the furthest boundaries of pleasure, boy. There is but a small difference between the two, one that is nearly impossible to distinguish until you've experienced it. I associate one with the other, physical pain with physical pleasure. What you fail to understand, however, is that I'm not laughing because of your feeble attempts to make me hurt or cause me pain, though I do find something about your method's rather…hilarious. It's more at the thought that you think you took me. You should know better than that."

The crows called again and Sam paused. Something she said, something about their *methods*, something about how they thought they had *taken* here. Suddenly, a concerned look covered his face.

The goddamn bird and the goddamn worm. Never be the worm. NEVER! This isn't good. It was all a fucking trick. She knew we were coming somehow. Fuck. We're about to be the worms.

The witch's head cocked to the side, watching Sam from the corners of her eyes. "You see, Anthony, I'm laughing at what your idiotic friend just realized, and perhaps at what he just remembered." She had a hint of playfulness in her voice. "You didn't forget something… important, did you?"

A horrible feeling ripped at Sam's chest as he looked to his friend. "I forgot about the fucking salt. Shit!" He rushed over to the bag and grabbed two full canisters of salt, tossing one to Anthony, who stared at it as if it were a bomb about to detonate.

"What? Wh-what are you talkin' about? You just used it on her! You just melted half of her fucking face off with it, Sam! Remember?"

"No, Anthony! This is not for her. It's for *them*."

The woman laughed as she rocked the chair back and forth.

"*Them*? *Them*, who?"

"Just listen to me, Anthony. We don't have much time. We...well, *I* fucked up. This is what she wanted all along, and there's too many of them now. That's why they've not been trying yet. They've been waiting. Fuckin' shit, I can't believe I forgot about it!"

"Too many of what?" Anthony looked at the woman and a wave of disgust filled his stomach. Her smile was sickening to him, that sadistic smile plastered permanently over her mouth.

"They're coming for you, Sammy. And they're *hungry!*"

Sam hit her again, then turned his focus back on Anthony. "Listen, I'm gonna go outside and make a circle around this place with the salt. It'll keep them away as long as they're under her command. They're just like her." He looked back at the woman. "If they try to cross it, it'll burn them, too. They won't even risk trying to fly over it, as long as it's complete, anyway."

Their calls came in waves now, each one a relentless scream of mockery.

"What? Wh-why?"

"It's a barrier. They can't cross it. It's the only thing that stayed consistent with all the witch stories I looked into. Trust me. You," he placed a hand on his friend's shoulder, "need to stay inside and make a line on the sill of each window and in front of each door. That way they can't come through if they do somehow manage to get around the outside. Got it?"

"Barrier? Barrier for who, Sam? I-I don't understand."

"Just do it, okay?" Sam screamed.

Anthony's eyes were wide, stretched to unnatural limits like those in the old Saturday morning cartoons. He nodded erratically, still not quite sure of what he was about to do, or why.

Something slammed into the back window. The sound reverberated throughout the cabin, bouncing off of every hard object it offered. A loud thud, a faint hint of splintering glass mixed in.

"Fuck! They've cracked one already. Start with that one, okay?"

The sound of hundreds of crows cawing echoed into the stillness of the night all around them.

"What the fuck is goin' on out there?" asked Anthony, fear slipping into his voice like some kind of unseen and otherworldly phantom.

The witch cackled. "They're here, boys. Are you ready? I think not!"

Sam pushed past Anthony and ran toward the door. "Just do it, Anthony. We'll be okay. And if one of them gets in, kill the motherfucker."

Another thud against the window, one against the side of the cabin. The birds were coming for them…for her, descending from the heavens in massive droves. The woman thrashed about madly as the large creatures slammed themselves into the walls and windows with reckless abandon, nothing more than dedicated servants obeying their wicked master.

"Don't listen to anything she says, remember that. Nothin'. Got it?"

"I-I…" Another bird slammed into the window, breaking his thought. "What the fuck do they want?"

Sam grabbed the shotgun with one hand, the doorknob with the other, a canister of salt under his arm. "They're here to save her, and they're here to kill us."

5

Sam pushed the door open and immediately crows began to swoop down, bombing him from every direction.

"Goddamn birds!" He covered his head and neck, defending the exposed skin from the likes of their razor-sharp beaks. But still, somehow, they found openings, and they sliced into his flesh. It wasn't until Sam fired the first shot sending a cascade of coal black feathers and spurts of blood into the air that he was able to finally catch his breath. The boom of the shot lingered in the air for what seemed like eternity, hanging on to every surface that allowed its reflection. He opened the canister of salt and began walking around the cabin, doing his best to pour an unbroken line on the ground as he went, while still looking to the sky for any sign of his attackers.

He couldn't hear them, but he knew that they were there. Crows, he'd heard on television, were very intelligent birds, and their intelligence would only be amplified by the magic of a witch. That, he hadn't heard on television, but it made sense given the current circumstances. He could feel their shiny black eyes watching him, studying his movements so that their the next attack would count. But why weren't they coming for him like before? It had to be the gun shot. *Had* to be. They'd met their match, he thought. She couldn't be killed like normal humans, but they could. They were nothing more than mortal animals, slaves ordered against their will to do evil upon the innocent.

He walked slowly around the first corner of the cabin, skirting along the side wall. As he neared the second corner, he heard something rustling above him. A single *caw* followed, one that unleashed the gates of Hell directly on him. He looked up and, just outside of arm's length, a crow stared back. Its eyes glistened against the moonlight, its beak held steady, hanging partially open.

Sam licked his parched lips. "Goddamn bastard birds," he whispered, and gently started to lift the barrel of the gun toward the demonic flock. He took a step to the side so that he could put enough room between himself and the bird to get a shot off, but it hopped to another branch. "Hold still, fucker," he said in a low voice. "I'm not gonna hurt you, not one, little, bit. I *promise*."

By the time he took the final step around the corner to allow enough room to clear the shot, it was too late. He lifted his foot, but it wouldn't move. Something was blocking it from shifting position. With the weight of his body already moving in the wrong direction, he fell backward to the ground. The shotgun slipped from his hand, its barrel jamming into the soft earth beneath him.

He landed with a dull thud that knocked his already shaken breath away. As he looked out into the darkness, he saw sparkles of light glistening before him. It was their feathers, the oil covering them shined in the moonlight like ocean waves glittering in the light of a distant shore. Much like those same waves move until they crash into the banks that contain them, the birds moved with determined force toward Sam.

"Jesus Christ," he whispered, pushing himself back against the cabin's wall. His heart began to race and, for the first time since his son had been taken away, he felt true

The Bird and the Worm

fear in his heart. *I'm not going to make it. We're going to die up here. I'm about to be the worms.*

There were hundreds of them, hundreds of the unholy beasts covering the ground like a gigantic black animated blanket. They swayed back and forth, their wings stretching to their sides as they hopped toward him, closer and closer until he lay pinned against the side of the structure.

He pushed himself up to his knees and clenched his fists, readying for the last fight. They might take him, but he would go out swinging. "Alright, come on! You want me so bad? Come and get me!" He lunged at them, attempting to force a reaction, but they remained still. They were not afraid, and he knew it. For them, there was no fear greater than that of the witch's wrath. There was only one way out. The gun was out of reach, and hordes of crows stood atop and around it, perched on its stock as it stuck from the ground like a rogue arrow. It was almost as if they were begging him to make a move for it.

Come on, Sam. You know you want to. You know you want to shoot us. Come and get it, see what happens, Sam. We can only imagine how delicious your flesh will taste as we're tearing it away from your bones. Come on, let's play a game.

Deep down, he knew the gun would be almost impossible to reach, that getting it was as near a death wish as he'd ever dared to go. The birds would tear him apart, no questions asked. There was only one thing left to do, and if he wanted it, he had to fight. He clenched his teeth and tensed his muscles. He looked around one last time for anything he could use as a weapon, and that's when he saw the canister of salt at his feet. A small sliver of hope found him and a surge of adrenaline flowed freely throughout his body. He looked out to the sea of crows and grinned.

"See how you devil birds like this one!" He reached down and grabbed the salt, flinging it out and sending a spray of the fine particles into the night like little weaponized pellets. The crows scattered, forming a crude arc in front of him. Some of the salt made contact with a few of the birds, those that were hit let out an unworldly cry unlike any he'd ever heard. "It works," he whispered. "It hurts them, too."

He looked to each side and based on how far he'd made it, knew that it would be closer to get to the front door than it would be to finish his trip around the cabin. At least there, he had shelter. They might get in, but he had something between him and them. He hurled a bit of salt against the wall and the crows scattered, allowing him a few feet of space.

He looked toward the first corner, then to the gun. The canister was running low and he had to make a choice – perhaps the most important one of his entire life to this point. If he went for the door, he could find safety inside. But for how long? If he went for the gun, he had enough shells to get off three shots, maybe, before having to reload, and there was no way they would let him reload without ripping him to shreds.

Fuck it. I'll go for the gun and blast the shit out of them until I get to the door. If they kill me, at least I'll take a few of them with me.

The crows had other plans. It was as if they'd heard his thoughts, listened to his plotting against them and realized that it was pitifully stupid. As he pulled his arm back and slung it forward to spill another round of salt, a

The Bird and the Worm

sharp pain pierced the back of his neck, then his ear, and then his hand.

"Jesus!" he yelled, falling forward to his knees. The canister of salt hit the ground and rolled just out of reach. The crows descended in front of him, blocking his way. He glanced up and into the eyes of one of the animals, its unforgiving gaze locking onto his.

He bit down, dug his feet into the soil, and swung his fist with all his might. The impact reminded him of someone dropping a head of lettuce onto the floor. It was a crunchy, almost spongy noise, the strike sending the bird through the air and into its kind. He lunged into the mass of birds and they quickly descended on top of him.

Sam's fingers dug into the earth as he pulled himself forward inch by inch. Razor sharp beaks sliced into his flesh cutting every patch of exposed skin down to bone, ripping his shirt from his back as he tried to sweep them off. He screamed, the pain as close to unbearable as he'd ever experienced, but he kept pushing forward, one hand at a time until his palm fell on something that didn't give, something that wasn't the soft, muddy earth. Instinctively, his hand clenched the object and flung it to his side.

It was the canister of salt, and he'd just spent the remainder of it.

Small particles of the precious mineral scattered into the air. It crashed into the birds causing a mixture of violent cries and sizzling hisses. It was a small moment of reprieve, but it was just enough. Sam threw his head up. At an arms-length away was the shotgun, a group of crows holding it with their claws. They were trying to pull it away.

Sam kicked his feet sending several of the beasts backward. He got to his knees and crawled toward the gun, blood flowing freely from all of the bite marks covering his body. He grabbed the gun just as the crows closed the distance and started tearing away at his legs again. Like a professional baseball player making the final attempt at a game winning home run, he yanked it from the mud and swung it into the small flock gathered at his feet.

The sound it made as it broke the bones of the damned birds sent a much-needed surge of hope his way. He stuck his fingers into the barrel, an attempt to quickly remove any dirt that may have jammed inside, then turned toward the door, pumped a shell into the chamber, and pulled the trigger.

The shot sent a mess of bloody feathers and flesh into the air. He stood up and shot again, then another. The path to the door was clear. He pumped the gun and realized that the next shot would be his last until he could reload, but he only needed one more shot to make it. Birds clawed as his shoulders from above and behind, scratching and tearing away at his body.

The bird and the worm. If the bird catches the worm…then it's…

"Fuck you! I'm not about to be your fucking worm!"

He swung around, aimed the gun, and took the last shot. A bluster of shiny feathers crowded the sky, and Sam dropped his hand over the handle of the cabin door.

6

With Sam gone, the room was quiet, minus the heavy breathing from Anthony and the old woman.

Anthony supposed that he may as well admit to himself that she was a witch at this point, but if he did that, he felt he would be letting go of his sanity, if there was any left to be had. That was something he couldn't afford to do. Not out here.

He glanced at her, she was still sitting in the corner. She returned his look with a sense of uncomfortable hate that he thought never possible. The way she stared at him, with a feeling of deep intent, made his insides squirm.

"Mmmm MMMM! Would you just *look* at this? What a treat!" She licked her lips hungrily. Her long, pointed tongue slipped between her grayed, cracked lips moistening the dried skin. She eyed him up and down in an almost lustful way. "Aren't you just, something?"

He looked away from her and took the salt to the first window, laying down a line on the sill as instructed.

"You don't really believe him, do you Anthony?"

He continued to work, diligently pouring the salt as he ignored the wit—no, the *old woman's* ranting.

"You can't honestly believe that I'm a…well, a *witch*, can you? Isn't all that magic and hoodoo talk supposed to be for children? You know, make believe and child's play?"

"Sh-shut up, woman. I'm not listening to you! I'm just not gonna listen," he replied nervously.

Her voice took a lighter, more familiar tone. "Look at me, Anthony. Please?"

Anthony froze. Her voice wasn't hers anymore, it wasn't the same evil, shrill hiss of someone he'd only moments ago considered to maybe be a witch. He recognized the tone, but he didn't want to look. If he did, and the person sitting in the chair was no longer the old woman, he'd be forced to admit one of two things. That the woman was, indeed, a witch, or that he'd lost his mind. He took a deep breath and the faint odor of vanilla slithered up into his nose.

No. It can't be, he thought. *Vanilla is...it's just impossible.*

"That's it," she continued. "You know you've been a bad boy, don't you, baby? You've done something really, really bad this time and you have to be punished for it."

"Shut up!" he yelled in protest. "I-I'm not listening to you. This isn't real!" He squeezed his eyes closed and shook his head, the sweet aroma of vanilla clinging to his nostrils like a fungus. "It's not *real*!" When he opened his eyes, his worst fear came rushing back to him. Instead of seeing the old woman, he saw the woman he'd heard in the new, familiar voice, sitting in the same old wooden chair in the same old dark corner. The same one the old woman had just been bound to.

He blinked, no more than a fraction of a second, and he was no longer in the cabin. The chair had changed, too. It wasn't rickety and ready to fall to pieces. There was no barbed wire holding the new owner's limbs in place. No old, evil sounding, gray haired demon woman strapped to its base. Instead, he was in the kitchen of his childhood home.

"No," he whispered. "There's no way this is real." His muscles tightened, locked into place as his mind tried to sort through the corrupt memories. "I-I don't want to remember this. It isn't real."

The woman before him had her legs crossed and her hands neatly placed on the chair arms. Her wavy blond hair draped over a slightly worn flower print dress. "You know what has to happen, Anthony. It's the only way to teach you," she said.

As the woman in the corner spoke to him, he noticed something strange about her lips, something about her voice. They were out of sync with each other, movements independent of sound. "Go on, now. Don't make your father any more upset than he already is. You remember the last time, don't you?"

He thought back to his younger days, to the time he'd accidentally knocked a glass of water over and ruined his father's favorite girly magazine. He'd beaten Anthony badly that evening, then thrown him into the basement for nearly three days before even checking on him.

Anthony's stomach dropped, the feeling of free fall consumed his body. He closed his eyes again, arms out to fight the growing dizziness. Once steadied, he opened his eyes and the new woman was still there, motioning for him to come to her. He tried to fight it. He didn't want to go, but his body was overriding the commands sent from his brain as he desperately fought for control. He clenched his fists, tried to pull away, but it was too much.

"M-Mommy…please don't make me do this again. I-it's scary down in there. It's too dark and…it smells funny."

She smiled, continuing to draw him closer. "It's okay, baby. One of these day's maybe you'll learn and we won't have to put you down there anymore. Does Mommy get her special *little* treat before you go this time?" She lowered her gaze to the zipper of his jeans and cocked one eyebrow. "It's been a little while, hasn't it? That's what happens when little Anthony is a bad boy."

"I-I don't wanna do that anymore, Mommy. P-please don't make me."

"Oh, now. You know that Mommy knows best. Isn't that right, baby?"

"Please, Mommy. Pretty please don't make me do that again. I-I don't want too."

"Well, I suppose we can let *that* part slide…*this* time. But, you have to do something else for me. Something very important. You know you've been naughty, and you must be punished. Before you go, come here and give Mommy a big hug. It'll make you feel better. I promise."

As he grew closer, Anthony realized that her face was blurry. It had been that way the whole time, he'd just not noticed it until now. It was as if she sat just out of the direct focus of a camera lens, an extra object in the background.

"Come on, now. Daddy's gonna force you if you don't do it on your own. You're getting too big to act like a little baby." She pointed to her side with her thumb, her arm never leaving the chair's arm.

Anthony turned his head and saw his father. A plume of smoke rising from his mouth as he puffed on a cigarette, a wide leather belt wrapped around his right hand as he squeezed it tight. "That's right, boy. Better do what your momma says or this one'll be even worse than the last. You done fucked up by beatin' an old woman, boy. You know better'nat."

"Beating an old woman?" Anthony whispered. "I-I didn't, did I?" His mind raced with confusion as the thoughts of his youth mixed with those of his adulthood. "N-no," Anthony said aloud. "Don't make me do it again, Daddy. Please don't make me do it again." He blinked, and suddenly he was in front of his mother. The distance had closed in less than a second, and he'd not even remembered moving that much. She was still out of focus, and it looked as if her image were trembling, shaking apart from the world. It reminded him vaguely of the television shows he'd watched with Sam as a child when the main characters jumped between two separate dimensions.

"Are you ready to help Mommy now with that special favor?"

He nodded, reluctantly.

"Good, boy. Help me up, would you? I can't seem to get to my feet for some reason. I guess I'm just getting old."

Anthony reached down and held his mother's wrists. He could feel something hard against them, hard and cold, but he could only see her milky white skin. He fumbled a bit, his hands running up and down her wrists, then her ankles, with no apparent purpose. He couldn't stop, though. No matter how hard he tried his hands made the strange motions up and down her limbs. He was moving against his own will, like a machine under the control of a computer.

"Thank you, dear. That's much better," she said, standing up and rubbing her forearms.

"I don't understand," he replied. "What happened?"

Suddenly, the room began to spin. Anthony's stomach became sick and his balance grew weak. He could feel himself falling backward, but he was falling into nothing, into emptiness. The sensation was strong and he prepared himself to land on the hard floor. Everything moved at an abnormally slow pace. He reached his hands out in an attempt to grasp something, anything to keep him from going down, to stop the overwhelming feeling of dread being forced upon him, but there was nothing there. He looked from side to side but could see only darkness. There was no furniture, no people – nothing but black.

When he finally landed, the surface he hit was soft. The jar of the impact forced his eyes shut, and this time when they opened, he was somewhere else altogether. He jerked to an upright position and scanned his surroundings. He was in a bed, the softness he'd felt had been a mattress. *His* mattress. He was in his childhood bedroom. Around him he saw his dresser, a small desk, and a chair. There was a closed door on one wall, a ragged basketball net suctioned to its back.

This is my old room. This can't be happening to me.

He heard yelling somewhere far away. His heart skipped a beat, just as it had when he'd heard the same argument as a child all those years ago. It was coming from another room, and he could tell that it was his mother and father.

"He's a goddamn pussy," he heard his father say. "Ain't nothin' else to be said about it. He's just a whiney little pussy. That's all. 'At boy ain't never gonna learn, neither. Probly gonna end up a lil' fag. I'm tellin' ya. Lock him in that goddamn basement till he's fuckin' grown for all I care. Goddamn little worthless shit."

He heard his mother giggle. "He's definitely not the strongest, that's for sure. But if you keep beating him like that, people are gonna start askin' questions. You know how people are, 'specially 'round here. And you've gotta stop pushin' him so hard if you wanna keep makin' the videos. He's gettin' to where he don't like it no more. I think he's startin' to figure out that it ain't normal."

"Pushin' him? Hell, Darla, people pay good money for them tapes. Why else you think I've kept him around for this long? Nah, I say we lock him down there. He won't be missed. It ain't like he's got any friends 'cept for 'at little queer he hangs around with from time to time. What's his name, again? Sam? He'll just disappear and ain't nobody ever gonna look for him. Even if they do, we could be long gone by the time they find him."

Anthony shook his head in disbelief. He'd escaped this place once, and he thought he'd never have to go back. Thought he'd never have to relive the nightmare again. Yet, here he was, all these years later, and he could smell the vanilla perfume his mother used to wear, the whiskey and smoke on his father's breath, just like he did when it happened the first time. He saw himself in a mirror hanging on the wall of his old bedroom and noticed that his face was bruised, a mixture of different shades of deep blues and purples. His eye looked to be nearly swollen shut and the familiar taste of metal filled his mouth. Yet, when he reached up to feel it, everything was normal. He looked at the mirror again, running his fingers across the battered image.

"It's not really happening," he whispered. He walked closer to the mirror and stared. "This...isn't real."

"Fuck it," he heard his father announce. "Throw him in the basement, give him a box of cereal or somethin' to eat that'll make him think we're gonna get him in a day or two, you know, like we always do. Then we'll just pack up and get the hell outta here."

His mother laughed again, almost playfully. "We can't do that." There was a long pause, and then he heard her continue. "Can we?"

"Fuck him. Survival of the fittest, right? And let's face it...'at boy ain't the fittest."

Anthony's breathing grew heavy. Hot, salty tears formed in his eyes and ran down the edges of his cheeks and into the corners of his mouth. He remembered the moment he'd first heard this conversation, word for word if memory served. It was the moment he'd realized his parents didn't care about him. To them, he'd been nothing more than an expendable end to make a quick and dirty dollar. Sam was his only friend. He was the only one he could turn to when his parents fled from his life after years of sexual, mental, and physical abuse left him dead inside, a mere shell of what a child should be.

A slight breeze ran across his neck filling his ears with a whisper. "You don't want to go back to that nasty, bug infested basement, do you Anthony?"

His eyes sprang open wide and he jumped around to see who was with him.

The room was empty.

"You tried once," the whisper told him. "Remember? The first time you heard all of this. You *almost* succeeded."

Anthony spun in the room. He knew that, logically, the voice had to have an owner. But there was nobody else there.

He heard his parents in the other room still, talking about their plans to leave him for dead, locked in the damp, dark hole in the earth beneath the house.

"You won't fail this time, Anthony. I won't allow it. I'll make sure you do it right. And I promise, you won't even feel a thing."

As if being ushered to his seat at some high class event, Anthony felt a presence surround him, pushing – no, helping – him toward the dresser. The top drawer opened by itself, and inside lay an old Case pocket knife he'd stolen from his father to get back at him for one of the beatings he'd dealt him.

I can't do this. I can't go through this shit again.

"Yes, you can," the whisper sang. It was tempting. Irresistible, like the sweet song of a siren dancing in his mind. "It's *easy*. Really. Just…*let go*."

Anthony's eyes burned as he fought the stream of tears cascading down his face. His lower lip quivered, the memories he'd pushed down for so long resurfacing with a vengeance. His mother molesting him, his father filming it to sell to the highest bidder. He stared at himself in the mirror and cried. "But…what about …"

His hand moved independently of his mind, opening the pocket knife, pressing the blade into his wrist.

"I-I can't. I have to help Sam. I *promised*. He *needs* me."

"For what? Are you really going to help him murder an old woman out in the woods? Why, you'll go to prison for that, Anthony. And think of what *they'll* do to you in there. Besides, he doesn't care about anyone but himself. Think about it. Where is he now? He's left you alone. All alone in this house with dear ol' *Mommy*." The sweet sound of the whisper in his ear, the smell of vanilla, strong and powerful, it was all too much. Maybe the voice was right. Maybe Sam didn't need him. Maybe he only cared about himself. The easy thing to do would be to just…give in.

"Bu-but he's the reason I'm still alive. I looked over and he was at my win—"

He felt a sudden pain in his wrist, one that jerked his mind back to the moment…back to reality. He looked down at his arm. In his hand was a piece of shattered glass from one of the broken windows. He had driven it into his arm, effortlessly slicing from wrist to elbow in a long, irregular path. "N-no," he stuttered. He grew dizzy as blood ran down his arm in a steady stream, coating the cabin floor. He staggered about on wobbly legs, bumping into furniture, into walls. Just as he thought he couldn't stand any longer, he crashed into something different, something soft, and he felt hands take hold of his shoulders.

"That's it, Anthony," the wicked voice whispered. "What a good boy you've been for Mommy."

He shook his head as he tried to clear the delusions from his mind. The old woman held him now. No, he thought finally. She was no woman. Sam was right. She was a witch. The beautiful blond hair replaced by the gray, stringy mess; the stunning face replaced by a sinister grin, one that allowed a rancid breath from between jagged and broken teeth. He tried to push her away, but her strength was too much for his weakened state.

The witch's grin turned into a smile that seemed too large for her face. She licked her lips hungrily as her

The Bird and the Worm

narrowed eyes looked into Anthony's. "Now, the real fun begins." She lay Anthony onto the floor and knelt above him. "You thought you captured me? Foolish, foolish boys. I allowed it, just like I allowed him to take the book before. This is all a game to me, one that I'm afraid you're about to lose. Your friend want's his precious Danny back so badly, hmm?"

Anthony struggled to make a sound, but only broken whines would come. The loss of blood was making him weaker as every second ticked by.

The woman chuckled. "It's okay, boy. I know he does. But, Danny's body is gone, you see? It's done gone and turned sour. I made certain of that. The both of you buried it in the earth two years ago with the rest of the worms and maggots. No way he's coming back now. Why, even if he did…it wouldn't be pretty. Hell, it'd take a magic stronger than mine to even make *that* happen."

Anthony continued to struggle, to force his muscles against their will.

"His soul, though, is very much alive. I have it, in fact. I keep it in a little vile on a shelf in my cellar, along with all the other children I feel are…*special*." She laughed. "Most, I eat. They keep me alive through the winter, you see? But the special ones," she ripped a piece of blood-soaked skin from Anthony's wound and licked it before tossing it into her mouth. "I use for…other purposes. I'm not the only one who loves the taste of innocence in these woods." She placed her finger in her mouth and sucked Anthony's blood from it. "Mmmm, delicious!"

Anthony took in shallow breath as blood continued to leak from the gash on his arm.

"It appears that you don't have much time left, either. What a pity." She reached down and rubbed her finger in the wound on Anthony's arm, ripping away another small chunk of his flesh, causing him to winced. "Oh! That hurt, did it?" She placed the small bit of meat into her mouth and began to chew. "It's a shame, you know, that you got dragged into all of this for a small, worthless little child."

A loud scream seemed to slice through the walls of the cabin, the witch's attention turning to the noise as an evil, almost concerned look fell on her as her crows called.

A loud blast, followed by another.

"Well, I do believe my time here has come to an end, wouldn't you agree? My birds are telling me that he's close, now. Do me a favor, would you…Anthony? Tell your buddy Sammy that if he wants his little bastard son's soul, he can come and get it himself. But he'd better hurry. Someone else wants it, now. And he's coming for it, soon."

A thunderous roar blasted across the room from the front door as it flew open. The witch leapt upward toward the ceiling, suspending in the air. Anthony twisted to look for her, and for a brief moment, he thought he could see her floating toward the sky, passing through the solid roof of the building as if she were some sort of ghostly hallucination; a black mist vanishing into the night.

The last thing he noticed was that horrid smile on her face, and just as she slipped away, Anthony's vision turned to black.

7

The door flew open and Sam fell inside, quickly slamming it shut behind him. The sounds of crows crashing into it made him cringe.

"Goddamn fucking birds!" He fumbled to his hands and knees, wiping a mixture of blood, dirt, and sweat from his face. "Those fucking things nearly ate me alive out there." He reached into the duffle bag on the floor next to him and grabbed an old rag, pressing it against his face. "But guess what, bitch? I got some of 'em. Blew 'em into little bitt—"

As he took the rag away from his face, the site of Anthony laying on the floor in a pool of blood startled him. He rushed over to his friend's side, careful not to slip in the crimson liquid. "Wh-what happened?" He saw Anthony's arm, the large sliver of glass still embedded deep inside the tissue, and realized it to be the source of the blood. "Jesus, what did you do, Anthony?" He ripped a thin strip away from his shirt and tied is above his friend's elbow, an attempt to slow the bleeding. "What did you—"

His thought was broken as a sudden feeling of terror engulfed him. The pit of his stomach lurched up into his throat as his senses heightened to near extraordinary levels. Something had happened, yes. And it was quite obviously something bad. But a question came to him, one that he couldn't help but ask himself. Anthony was there, and so was he. But where was the witch?

Slowly, his head turned to the corner where the she had been sitting in the chair before he went into battle with the crows. The chair was still there, but it was empty now, crumpled strands of rusted barbed wire laying on the ground beneath.

"Anthony," he whispered, his eyes never leaving the corner. "Where is she?"

An odd sound flittered through the air. All around them, something akin to laughter, but more demonic and sinister, began to fill the room. It fell from the trees, surrounding them in the overwhelming presence of evil.

Except, it wasn't laughter. Sam recognized it, the cawing and squawking, mockery at its finest. It was the crows, and they were calling to each other in ways that weren't normal for any bird to call.

"Sh-trck me," Anthony murmured, voice strained and fading. "Y-you-rgt."

Sam felt a weak pressure against his arm as Anthony tried to grasp his wrist. "What did she do to you? What happened in here?"

Anthony raised his head a few inches from the floor, glanced at the glass in his arm. "Y-you re-mber that…b-basement? Y-you-th-reason…I-I—"

"We've gotta get you to a hospital, man," Sam said, interrupting. "Otherwise, you're gonna die. Ain't no two ways about it." He looked around the room. Broken glass lay on the floor. Blood pooled around them. The sounds of the crows echoed outside, beckoning them to come out and play.

"I-it's wh-at she wanted. Trick. Sh-she has…him."

Sam's eyes widened, his mouth fell open as Anthony struggled to tell him what he knew, what he'd been told by the witch.

"What did you just say?"

"She knew…ev-eryth-ing. She ha-s…she has… Danny."

Sam grasped his shoulders, his face coming only inches from Anthony's. "H-he's alive? He can't be. You, saw him? Anthony, did you see Danny?"

He could see the desperation in his friend's eyes, a sadness that lurked deep within a long-ago shattered heart. He shifted position slightly as he tried to prop himself up on his elbow, trembling under his own weight. "N-no. Not…h-he-re."

Sam's eyes glazed over and his lips curled downward. His entire body stiffened as the small sliver of hope he'd just been given came crashing down.

"B-but," Anthony continued. "H-is…s-oul. I-it's with…her."

"His soul? She has it? That means there *is* still a chance."

"His…body." He coughed, his body weak, head weaving back and forth. "Sh-e said that…h-is body's gon-g-gone…s-sour. She s-said that…s-someone else wants it." As he finished the sentence, Anthony closed his eyes, falling unconscious.

Sam slapped his face gently, trying to get him to respond. "Anthony. Anthony, stay with me, man." He placed two fingers on his neck and found a weak pulse. "You're not dying on me, Anthony. It's not happening. Not out here, and not like this."

He took the shotgun and stuffed it full of shells before throwing the duffle over his shoulder. He grabbed Anthony and dragged him up against the wall.

"Okay man," he said, slapping him across the cheek again. "I know it's tough, but you're gonna have to help me."

Anthony's eyes flickered open and shut again.

"You can do this. I know you can. Remember that basement? You wanted to die then, and I wouldn't let you. Your parents left you, Anthony, but I didn't, and I'm not goin' to now. But I can't get you out of here alone. Not with them goddamn crows comin' at us from every direction."

"B-base-ment," Anthony stuttered.

"Can you do that for me? Can you help me, just a little, so we can make it to the truck?"

Anthony's head moved, his eyes opened to look into Sam's. "I-I'm notgna mait." His eyes glanced to his arm, to the pool of blood on the floor. "Lost too much. Too late. Hsptl too far."

Sam knew that Anthony was probably right. If he didn't do something fast, he was going to die. His eyes were drooping, their deep greem color and glossy shine fading away. His breathing was shallow and weak, his face as pale as chalk. But he couldn't give up on him. Not yet. He loved him like a brother, he had ever since they were kids. They'd went through everything together, all the way up until Danny's death when Anthony helped put his body in the ground. But there was another reason he couldn't let Anthony die. A more selfish one. If he wanted to get Danny back, he needed his help. He needed to know what the witch had said. All of it.

Dad was right. The bird and the worm, he thought. *That fucking bitch. There's no other choice, now. It's the*

The Bird and the Worm

only thing left to do. He's gonna die if I don't. I've gotta at least try.

He grabbed Anthony under the shoulders and heaved. "Nope. It's not too late, and we're not goin' to a hospital. We're not about to be the worm in this story, Anthony. Remember that? Dad used to say it all the time. You're gonna live through this, but you've gotta want it. You've gotta fight and keep on goin', just like that poor little worm has to."

Anthony staggered for footing, finally forcing himself to stand as he propped against Sam.

"That's it," Sam grunted, struggling to hold his weight. "Hold on and just do the best you can. We're gonna get outta here. I promise you that."

The truck was only a hundred or so feet from the front door, but the fact that they would be moving slower due to Anthony's current condition made things even more dangerous. He could hear the crows mocking them from the treetops. They were waiting, and he knew it, but he only needed one chance.

He grabbed the handle of the door and flung it open. Immediately, the birds came for him, biting and scratching at his face. He pointed the gun and pulled the trigger. Feathers flew into the night like shrapnel from an explosion, scattering the birds in every direction. He dragged Anthony a few feet, then took another shot. With each blast, the birds scattered just enough for them to gain a few feet. They wouldn't get to the truck unharmed, but that was okay. They just needed to get there alive.

With one final shot, Sam took out several of the birds. He managed to open the passenger door and lay Anthony in the seat, birds pecking at his head and neck the entire time. He closed the door and as he turned, a small group of the savage animals ripped at the exposed skin on his neck. He reached his hand around and took the offending bird in his grip, bringing it to his front and into his vision. He looked into its eyes, empty and hollow. The bird scratched with its clawed feet, flapped its wings in protest as several more of the wild animals pounded into him.

He pointed the gun into the air with his free hand and fired, giving him a momentary reprieve from the onslaught. Looking into the bird's eyes, he smiled. "Find yourself another worm. And when you get to hell, you make sure and tell that ol' bitch that I'm comin' for my boy, and I'm gonna end her once and for all." He squeezed with all his might, relishing the feeling of bones crunching under his power. He squeezed until he couldn't squeeze anymore, until his muscles reached the pinnacle of their strength and stamina, and finally he felt the thick, hard snap of a larger bone against his palm. The bird quivered and went limp. Sam hurled the lifeless body into the darkness as he ran around and got into the driver's seat.

He looked at Anthony, his color paler still. "Hold on for just a little longer, Anthony. Just about forty-five minutes should do it. I think I know somebody who can help. If they're even real, that is. We've just gotta make it over to Caldwell's Mountain."

"N…no," Anthony stuttered in a broken whisper. "Nee…d-hsptl. Not real. She's j-just a stor-y…" His voice trailed off as he passed out in the seat.

Part II:

Old Folktales

8

February, 1990

Sam and Anthony sat in the living room floor in front of Sam's father, giving him their undivided attention. It was story time, after all, and there was nothing they loved more than a good old-fashion scary tale. Especially when Sam's dad was the one telling it. Some people just have a knack for storytelling, and old Appalachian folktales were Mr. Fletcher's specialty.

"Here's a good one for you boys," his father said. "And the best part is, it's *true*." The old man smiled and widened his eyes, playing the story up as best he could to try and scare the youngsters. "Long ago, there was a man who lived in a cabin a couple ridges over in Caldwell Junction. His name was Peter Caldwell, but everybody 'round there just called him Pete. He was the man who owned the whole town, matter of fact. He also owned a large piece of the land that surrounded it, including Caldwell's Mountain."

Sam and Anthony looked at each other, excitement in their eyes.

"Well, one day, a coal company came in and made Mr. Caldwell an offer on all of his land. You see, there was a big ol' coal seam that ran underneath it, and there was millions to be made if they could just dig it out. Mr. Caldwell wanted nothing to do with it though, so he turned the offer down." He smiled at the boys and shook his head. "You imagine that? Turnin' down millions of dollars?

That'd be tough, huh boys? Just think of all the things you could buy with a million dollars."

They laughed at the joke, but couldn't help but think of all the things they actually *could* buy if they had that much money to burn.

"That coal company, though, they really wanted his land, so they kept pushin' ol' Pete. Greed's a curious thing, boys. Don't ever let it get the best of you. They offered more and more money, sure that Mr. Caldwell, like most civilized people, had a price. But it turns out that everybody *but* Mr. Caldwell could be bought. He told 'em time n' time again that he didn't want nothin' to do with sellin' his land."

"Man," Anthony said. "I'd take that price for a mountain, wouldn't you Sam?"

Sam shrugged. "Maybe. That's a lot of money, for sure. I guess it depends."

"That it is, boys. That it is," Sam's father said with a sigh. "Be set for life. He'd been better off if he had've, too. See, the company *really* wanted that land, and they was willin' to do whatever it took to get it."

"What happened?" Sam asked.

"You boys sure you can handle it? I mean, it gets pretty rough from here on out."

Anthony looked at Sam and they both smiled. "What you think we are Mr. Fletcher, a couple of babies?"

Sam's father let out a boisterous laugh. "Okay, but I don't want either y'all wakin' me up in the middle of the night about it cause you're scared of what I'm 'bout to say and don't wanna go to the bathroom by yourself. Understand?"

They both nodded in agreement.

"Okay, then. Well, the way the story goes is, it was his family they went after; his wife and his young daughter. The bigwigs of the coal company hired a small group of real mean men to go into his house one night and kill his wife. They made him watch, too. Horrible sight, they say. They didn't kill her fast. All the stories say that they cut her into pieces while she was still alive. And if that wasn't bad enough, they took his daughter and told Mr. Caldwell they'd kill her if he didn't sign over the deed to the land. So, he signed it." He looked at the boys, lips pursed. "Can't say I blame him either. I'd do the same for either one of y'all."

"That's sayin' a lot," Anthony joked. "You ain't even my dad!"

"Is too," Sam protested. "He is now anyway. Same as."

"Right," Sam's father continued. "You're just as much my boy as Sam, here. But, back to the story. There was a little problem with their deal. After Mr. Caldwell signed the land over to 'em, they went on and slit that little girl's throat anyway, right in front of him!" He straightened up in his chair, his hands raised into the air for effect. "Said it was a lesson in negotiation, one he shoulda learned in the beginnin'."

"That's not nice," Sam said.

"Yeah. That's just…evil," Anthony seconded.

"That's not all, though. Here's where the real bad stuff starts to happen. The real weird and creepy part. Mr. Caldwell wanted revenge, and 'round here, in the mountains you know…they's a different kind of revenge. It's easy enough to go shootin' up a neighbor and throwin' 'em in a mountain break somewhere they won't never to be seen again, but when you're dealin' with a big ol' company with all that power and real deep pockets, that just won't work. You need a little somethin' extra. Sometin' to even the playin' field, as they say. Somethin'…supernatural, even."

"Here we go," Sam said enthusiastically. "Now we're gettin' somewhere."

"See, there's an old superstition 'round these parts. People like to laugh most of 'em off, but the superstitions about these kinds of things, they don't laugh about. Everybody thinks that these ones is real."

"Wh-what kinds of things," Anthony asked.

Sam's father looked at them, eyes squinted, and leaned in close. "*Witches*," he whispered. "And I ain't talkin' 'bout no wicked witch of the west, neither. I mean, *real* witches. The kinds who do black magic and have dealins with the devil and all that jazz."

"Ooohhh," Anthony said.

"They's three kinds of 'em 'round here that you gotta watch out for. They's good ones, evil ones, and ones that sort of just…are. The good ones, you see, they help cure people and such. Most people call them ones *holler witches*. They usually get along with everybody else. Kinda like them ol' Indian witch doctors. The mean and evil ones, well, they're the ones like in the movies you've seen. You know, things like them ol' boo hags and stuff, 'cept they're real, and in their truest form, they ain't too perty. Them's the ones who mostly deal with the devil and steal people's kids and all. The black magic ones." He looked at the boys and grinned. "They's one of 'em lives up on the hill just behind us, if I was tellin' the truth!"

The boys jumped back and laughed.

"No there's not! Stop that!" Sam protested.

"They ain't no witch up there," Anthony said. "We've been up there a bunch of times."

His father laughed. "No, not anymore they ain't, I guess. Used to be, though, 'till a bunch of people in town run her off. She was a mean old woman, too. Why, my grandpa used say that she liked to keep the souls of little kids in old mason jars, I reckon. She'd eat some of 'em, but the real special ones he said she'd keep for somethin' called, the one who walks in darkness. Best I can tell, that was supposed to be another name for Satan or somethin'. At least, that's what they say."

The boys looked at each other, terrified.

"But, you gotta remember, these is just stories, boys. Don't get too scared." He winked at them and smiled. "The last kind of witch, the one's that just sort of just…are, them's the ones with *real* bad powers. They don't gotta rely on spells and potions and things like that. Everybody says that they existed even before the lord God himself, it that's even possible. Why, them's the ones that Satan don't even mess with. Now if that ain't bad, I don't know what is. Ain't that right? Imagine somethin' so old that it was here before God, and so mean that the devil won't even go near it."

"That's pretty bad," Anthony agreed.

Sam nodded his head. "Yeah, I wouldn't want anything to do with that kind of person."

"Me neither. But, Pete let his anger and grief get the best of him, an that's the kind of witch he called on. Legend says that she ain't got a name, not a real one anyways. Everyone just called her the bone lady. See, in times of extreme need, when nothin' else worked, old timers say she could be conjured up. Brought about outta nothin'. Y'all understandin' me?"

"Sure," the boys said in unison.

"She was a sort of, fixer. Some people believed she could fix things that couldn't be fixed no other way. They say she had strong powers. The kind that could bring people back from the dead. Not everybody believed that part though, and that's where some people still yet argue about the whole thing. But if anybody other than God himself could do it, I reckon it'd be her. She didn't do nothin' for free, though. Get my drift?"

"What did it cost him? Mr. Caldwell, I mean," Sam asked, his interest in the story peaking. "He wanted his daughter back...right?"

"Well, of course he did. He wanted revenge for what them men had done to his family. But he had to make a sacrifice to get that. The bone lady was a collector of certain...*things*. People said she never got any older, and it was believed by most that she was able to do it by gettin' these collectibles. If you could give her what she needed, she'd use her dark powers to bring about justice for you. And Mr. Caldwell felt he deserved it."

"What kind of things did she collect," Anthony asked. "Like, what did she want from Mr. Caldwell as payment?"

Sam's father looked at Anthony, one-hundred percent seriousness on his face. "They called her the bone lady for a reason. She collected the bones of children. They say she had piles upon piles of bones, some of 'em stretched back to the dawn of civilization. Apparently, she liked to chew on 'em like an old dog. Not sure why that was the case though, people can make up some crazy stories, and I never met her to ask!"

"Uhhh, this is getting a little weird," Sam said.

"Yeah? We ain't even to the best part yet!"

Anthony reached over and gripped Sam's arm and they both gulped.

"Mr. Caldwell summoned that ol' bone lady to his house alright. But the problem was that he didn't have no bones to feed her. No bones except those of his dead family. So, he had a choice to make. He could either go on an bury his girl and live with it for the rest of his life; he could go out and get the bones of another innocent kid to give her so she'd bring his daughter back, or he could offer her bones up as payment for revenge. He wanted it so bad that it was killin' him inside, but he just couldn't bring himself to bring onto someother family the same kind of pain he was feelin. So, he did the next best thing. He went and fed that ol' bone lady the dead body of his daughter so that she could unleash a demon straight from Hell on them men."

"R-really?"

"That's what they say. I reckon it took ever one of 'em back down to Hell with it, too. And you know what? I think tonight's supposed to be a full moon."

"Wh-what about it?" Sam asked. "What about the full moon?"

"Yeah," Anthony repeated. "What's that got to do with anything?"

Sam's father grinned. "Well, the way most people tell it, when the bone lady brought that demon up, she made it to where it'd come back every full moon just to make sure nothin' was goin' on with Mr. Caldwell's land. That ol' demon comes out and roams the hills every time they's a full moon, you see? Still to this day." He laughed in a maniacally sinister, exaggerated laugh. "Just hope it don't come down this way."

"Dad!" Sam screamed. "That's not real! Tell us it's not real!"

"Now, if I'm bein' honest, I can't tell you it's real… but I can't tell you it ain't, neither. Just because I didn't see it don't mean it ain't real. But I'll tell you both one thing for certain."

"Yeah?" they responded.

"Even though them's just stories…folktales, really, if anything ever happens to either of you, and revenge is on your mind, don't go lookin' for that ol' bone lady. That ol' witch ain't somethin' you ever need to mess with. Understand? She's darker than ol' Lucifer, and she don't do nothin' for free. Besides, revenge is a dangerous thing. It'll warp your thinkin', make you do things you know better about. Got it?"

Both boys nodded, still excited and slightly nervous from the story. Neither of them knew whether or not to believe the old folktale, but one thing they did know…it was a good one.

9

December, 1990

The boys had just finished dinner when they overheard Sam's parents talking about a story they'd heard on the evening news earlier in the evening. As soon as he heard the word, Sam's interest piqued. He raised a hand to Anthony, hoping to get him to be quiet. He was going on about the latest issue of some comic, and Sam wanted to eavesdrop a little. Turns out that's hard to do when you can't hear.

"What," Anthony whispered. "Who cares about the news, anyway?"

"Listen, man. I think I heard Dad say somethin' about a witch."

Anthony's face grew bright with excitement. "Really? Like, a real one?"

They crept closer to the doorway leading to the kitchen and huddled against the wall. With each word his parents uttered, they listened with focused attention, the way a CIA agent does when trying to decode a top-secret message from a foreign spy. They heard something about 'witch', and then something about 'the hill behind the house', then something that sounded like 'Gunrack'.

Sam grasped Anthony's arm and took a deep breath. "Did you hear *that*?" he whispered. "They're talking about Gunrack Holler!"

Anthony was silent, still trying to listen.

"Dude...they're talking about a witch up Gunrack. A real one! That's just a few minutes from here! Only a couple ridged over!"

There was a pause in the conversation that forced the boys to creep a bit closer into the doorway to hear, so close that when Sam's father flung the door open it scared them senseless.

"And what do you boys think you're doin?"

"I-I-w-w-we were..."

"Is she real?" Anthony said. "You know, the witch up Gunrack?"

"Anthony!" Sam said.

His father looked at them both, eyebrows raised. "So, you all was eavesdroppin', huh? You know that ain't nice, right?"

Sam tried to speak, but he was too frazzled.

"Y-yes Sir," Anthony said. "But, we thought we heard you say somethin' about a witch up Gunrack. I-Is it true?"

Sam's father looked at them both and sighed. "Listen, boys. I told you that them was just stories. Sometimes, bad things happen. Somethin' bad happened to a couple of kids in town last night, but it was because they didn't listen to their parents. Understand?"

Sam shifted his eyes to the floor. "What happened?"

"Oh, a couple of youngins just got lost and couldn't find their way back home. Police found 'em froze to death this mornin'. That ain't got nothin' to do with no witch, though. These mountains and hollers, they're hard to navigate. 'Specially this time of year when it starts to get dark. One minute you can be on a hill somewhere, you go down into the holler to get to the next ridge, and next thing

Old Folktales

you know the daylight's gone. That's why I'm always tellin' you all to be good and mind me and your momma."

"But, what about the witch?" Anthony asked. "Y-you said it, we heard you."

"Yeah, Dad. I heard it too."

He shifted his weight from one foot to the other and sighed, hesitantly. "Well, I was just tellin' your momma that the way people 'round here are, they'll probably blame it on one. That's all. Besides, them's just scary stories. Remember?

"Yeah, but…" Sam started.

"But nothin'," his father said. "Y'all get on outta here before one of them witches that ain't real comes and gits you!" He laughed, motioning them away. "Go on up to your room and do somethin' fun, now. And stop eavesdroppin'."

10

January, 1991

As soon as he woke up, Sam knew something was wrong. He'd not even gotten the chance to stretch when the feeling hit him. That strange, creepy feeling, the kind you get when even the air seems different, like a wave of sorrow washing over the world.

He raised up in his bed and looked around the room. Anthony was still asleep in the bed across from him, and he heard the muffled sounds of what he thought to be someone crying coming from somewhere beyond the door.

"Anthony! Wake up, man. Somethin's wrong."

Anthony stirred a bit and pulled the blanket up over his head. "Whaisit man," he mumbled. "Go backaslp."

"Anthony!" he yelled, and threw a pillow at him. "Somethin's happened!"

Anthony slowly raised up and wiped his eyes. "What are you talkin' about?"

"Listen. Somebody is cryin' in the other room. Don't you hear it?"

Anthony yawned and focused his hearing. "I mean, I hear *somethin'*. Don't mean it's someone cryin'."

"No, man. I just...I have a feelin'. Somethin' doesn't feel right, you know?"

"Yeah, like gettin' up early on a Sunday mornin'." Anthony got out of bed and started toward the bathroom. He opened the door and the sounds of Sam's mother crying filled the room. He turned back to Sam. "Dude, your mom is crying at the kitchen table…and the police are in there with her."

Sam's stomach sank as he jumped up and ran to his mother's side. "Mom, what's wrong?" He looked around for his father, but he wasn't in the room. "Wh-where's Dad?"

She raised her head from the table, her face contorted into a hideous sight, a mess of snot and tears pouring down her cheeks. She sniffed, then began to sob again uncontrollably.

Sam's eyes opened wide as adrenaline spilled into his bloodstream. "Mom, what's wrong?"

One of the policemen reached over and hugged him. "I-I'm sorry, Sam. I'm afraid that your father has—"

Sam felt his heart fall a thousand miles. He didn't know exactly what the policeman was saying, but he knew that the end result would be the same no matter the words that came from his mouth. Something had happened to his father. He knew it. He collapsed to the floor and joined his mother in crying. Anthony rushed in and hugged him, crying himself.

The police told them that Mr. Fletcher had been deer hunting when he had an encounter with what must've been a bear. Bear attacks weren't common in Kentucky, but they happened occasionally. Nobody in town ever said much about it, though, and in the course of a few months the incident had largely been forgotten – chalked up to another hunting accident. Every time Sam would ask an adult about his father, they would just smile and abruptly change the subject as if avoiding the topic. He tried to ask his mother, the policemen, his father's friends, but nobody wanted to talk about it. It was like everyone in town was afraid to even mention it.

The notion that it had something to do with the missing children a month earlier, that a witch somehow had something to do with everything, floated around in Sam's mind for a bit, but he needed proof, and nobody wanted to talk about it. Sam wasn't ready to let it go just yet, though.

11

The first piece of evidence Sam collected came on a cool spring evening nearly five years after the death of his father. Sam and Anthony jumped off the school bus, intent on going fishing for the remainder of the evening. Sam grabbed the newspaper from the mailbox out front as he passed. He started toward the house to give it to his mother, like he typically did, but as he ran past Anthony, trying to be first, he dropped it on the gravel driveway. It landed, frontpage up, and the headline immediately caught his attention. He picked it up, stood in the driveway next to Anthony, and read it.

A group of campers had been found dead just a few miles from Gunrack holler, and according to the story, authorities were calling it a bear attack.

Bear attack, he thought. *How did a black bear kill five people? Not even one survived.*

That was the second alleged bear attack in his hometown in the last five years. Not something anyone would call normal for a small eastern Kentucky town.

From that point, the thought wedged into his mind that something was going on. Witch or no, something other than bear attacks were happening in the mountains around his home. Sam collected every clipping, every news story, and every shred of gossip he could manage from anywhere within twenty miles of town, focusing on anything to do with a strange murder or disappearance. There were quite a few occurrences, more than anyone liked to admit, but most were the result of deaths from addicts or drunk drivers doing what they do best. There were murders over prescription pain pills, meth overdoses, and even one case where some idiot got high on God knows what, locked himself inside of his house because he thought he was Jesus, and shot anyone that got close to him in the head while screaming, "I am your salvation! Repent and be free of all your sins!"

But there were some that didn't fit the bill as 'normal', at least in Sam's eyes. There was the disappearance of the little Jenkins girl in August of 1999. She'd been playing in her backyard when she disappeared. Her mother went out to get her for dinner and she was nowhere to be found. It was like she'd just vanished into thin air.

Then there was case of Tim Jude in September of 2001. Tim was twelve years old. His father was out in the yard with him when he turned away to flip some burgers on the grill. When turned back just a few seconds later, Tim was gone. The only remains were his clothes laying in a pile where he had been standing only moments before.

Both of these children were still missing to this day.

In total, Sam had collected six cases of strange or unusual disappearances around town. One thing that made them even more strange, was that they all occurred within a mile or so of Gunrack Holler. He presented the evidence to Anthony, but he wanted nothing to do with it. He'd told Sam that it was strange, but strange shit happens all the time, especially in small towns. He'd told him that witches were just the things of old mountain stories…folktales. He told him that he was just wastin' his time and that he should be more focused on girls.

Eventually, Sam realized that Anthony was probably right. They were getting older now, and maybe he was just too tied to the thought that something else happened to his dad; maybe he was just too attached to let it go. As time went on, Sam thought less and less about the disappearances, and as time does with all things, the memories faded away, forgotten and deemed nothing more than more than a childish investigation into the paranormal, left to history as clippings in an old shoebox.

After all, witches were just the products of make believe. Nothing more than old folktales.

Part III:

The Bone Lady

12

As the truck made its way down the old dirt mountain road, Sam felt his head slam against the roof countless times. The road was filled with ruts and potholes. It wasn't made for the kind of speeds he was traveling, but he was on a mission. It wasn't only about Danny, now. It was about his best friend, too.

He glanced at Anthony for a moment. His body lay slumped below the passenger's seat, his legs crumpled into the floorboard. "Hold on just a few more minutes, Anthony. Don't let go yet, we're almost there." He reached over and placed his hand on his friend's chest, feeling for movement, but the roughness of the ride made it impossible to tell if what he was feeling was Anthony's breathing.

His eyes back on the road, Sam noticed that the night was calm now. It was a stark separation from the unreal circumstances that they'd just witnessed and been a part of. Everything from the relentless cawing of the crows to the evil, sickening mind games the witch had used to nearly kill them both. At this one moment in time, the calmness seemed almost surreal to him.

He heard a wet sort of gurgle from the passenger seat, and he looked over just in time to see Anthony's chest rise. It was slow, up and down with each shallow breath, but he was still alive. And that, at least, was a good thing. He wouldn't make it much longer, though. Not if they didn't find some help. He'd lost too much blood, and he was still bleeding. The slick red streaks on the faux leather truck seat served as evidence.

Ahead, the bright beams from the headlights illuminated a fork in the road. Sam slammed on his brakes bringing the truck to a stop just before the split. He took a careful look to the right. The path looked easy and clear. In that direction, the road went downhill and it was wide and easily traversable. That fork would take them off the mountain, drop them down into Big Branch just shy of its intersection with Mt. Preston Road. There were *people* in that direction, houses, the hospital. Civilization. But all of that was still nearly thirty minutes away, and that was after they made it to the main road.

He looked in the other direction, toward the left fork. There, the road went straight across the ridge. It was narrow, and it looked as if it had been centuries since it was last traveled. That, Sam thought to himself, was very likely a safe assumption. It was cluttered in thick matts of tangled, recurved briars, a near impenetrable fortress of thorns. If the road were in decent enough shape, they could push through the wall of vegetation and be across the ridge in ten minutes or less.

But nothing was for sure once you traveled over there, over onto Caldwell's Mountain. That particular mountain had existed, to Sam at least, permanently suspended in another time. Perhaps that was nothing more than the product of a mixture of stories and young imaginations fueled by his father's tales. Perhaps not.

There were no hospitals along that road, no people or houses for as long as the road went on. Just an old abandoned shack from years past that lay hidden somewhere deep in the aged woods. Very few visitors set foot on Caldwell's Mountain, and those that did rarely lived to tell about it. The stories had always pushed the existence of a large, bipedal, demon-like beast that guarded the property, coming out every full moon to correct and punish those who dared trespass on the land. The moon wasn't full tonight, but it was damn close, and you know what they say, close only counts in two things: horseshoes and hand grenades.

Sam reached over and gripped Anthony's hand tightly. "I'm sorry, Anthony, but you wouldn't have survived the ride to the hospital. She's the only thing that can save you now." He swallowed hard and let his foot off the brake, turning the wheel to the left. The truck slowly crept toward the fork leading across the ridge.

The first few feet went easy.

The beginning of the road had been kept clear, probably because of the proximity to the intersection, but it wasn't long until Sam started to hear branches from the overgrown forest scraping the windows and smacking into the sides of the truck. The racket it made was steady, almost methodical in nature, as if something more than just branches scratched at the steel. It sounded more like it was something with a purpose, an agenda, fingers tickling them lightly wanting to play. He tried to look out the windows, but the darkness mixed with the encroaching vegetation, hugging over the truck like it meant to eat them, made it impossible to see. He pressed the brake again, coming to a stop, knowing that when he stopped the trees wouldn't scratch or slap into them anymore. Then, if the noise continued, his notion that the sounds were the product of something other than the trees, something…supernatural, *had* to be right.

Dead silence.

Slightly relieved, Sam looked around and started to ease his foot from the brake, when…

Crash!

Something smashed into the back windshield.

Sam jerked around quickly and saw a thin smear of blood across the outside of the glass.

Crash! Crash!

He jumped back, surprised by the things smashing repeatedly into the window. The darkness made it hard to tell what it was, so Sam turned to the side view mirror hoping for a better view. As his eyes fell on the glass, the source of the crashes became clear. A large crow sat atop the side view, head cocked at an angle, mouth hanging open as if starved to near death for a drink of cool water.

Sam gasped.

Another crash from the back, followed by one from the side, then several from the front and top. The crows had caught up to them, and they were ready with razor sharp beaks that could easily tear into the boys' soft flesh. They cut through the thick vegetation with ease, no regard for the briars that tore at their feathers as the continuously bashed into the glass. The force was so hard that the driver's side and back windows were beginning to crack from impact.

We're not going to be your victims! He thought. *Not. Gonna. Be. The goddamn. Worms!*

He took his foot off the brake and nearly plunged the gas pedal through the floor. The truck slung forward like a rocket, crashing into the thickest mass of briars yet. Somehow, the crows remained, clinging to every surface that their sinister little claws could grip, pecking away like a swarm of rabid beasts hungry for human flesh.

His mind raced, the only thoughts it held being those of his and Anthony's ultimate demise. *They're just gonna keep following us. There's no way to get away from them. They'll kill us no matter what! Sh-she's too powerful.*

He glanced ahead. The road continued to get tighter and tighter. Maybe the vegetation would eventually pluck the murder of crows away, he thought. Just maybe. Branches flung along the sides of the vehicle, the top sounding as though the trees themselves were attempting to rip it away. But the goddamn birds' grips seemed fiercer than their taste for blood. His focus ahead of him now, Sam saw that the road disappeared into a wall of tangled vines and shrubs. The vegetation had claimed the entire path, grown up and taken it back from the control of the alien human race.

At that moment, two options occurred to Sam: 1) brake hard and hope for the best in their fight against the demonic avian flock; 2) floor it and burst through the plant wall in hopes that there was, indeed, a trail on the other side and not a sheer drop-off leading over the mountain. Either way, he thought, their chances of getting out of this were about the same.

He gritted his teeth, gripped the steering wheel like his life depended on it, and floored the pedal. He squeezed his eyes closed just before impact. The sound of branches snapping filled the air like the popping of fireworks on Independence Day as the truck forced its way through the mountain barricade.

At first, Sam was sure that he'd made the right decision. The truck was going through! They were going to make it! But just as his mind had allowed a small sprig of hope to take root, the vehicle lurched to a hard and abrupt stop. Sam flew forward into the windshield. Anthony slammed into the passenger dash, his body limp and flinging freely like an old worn out dish rag.

Sam's head throbbed. He pressed his hand against it and found that there was no blood. That was good. There was, however, a sizeable knot already starting to rise. He pushed himself back and checked on Anthony. He was no longer breathing, or if he was, Sam couldn't find the rise and fall of his chest. He began to panic. "I'm sorry, Anthony," he said, his heart racing as the thought that he'd let his best friend die crept to the surface of his reality. "I-I should've…"

He bit down hard on his lower lip and the sharp pain forced the feeling of failure away, but his emotions overwhelmed him. Tears gathered just above his lower eyelids, creeping gently from the corners of each eye and down over his cheeks.

He looked out the windshield and saw that the truck was angled down toward the ground. It took him a moment to figure it out, but he was finally able to see enough to determine that he'd ran into a deep rut that looked to have been cut across the road just on the other side of the plant barrier. To his sides, he saw that the forest was open. He was no longer inside of the thick mess of tangled understory. The road looked to continue on, as well, but it was hard to tell for how long. The shine of the headlights offered little help at this point, as their beams were confined mostly to the ditch he'd driven into.

He looked around frantically, confusion and shock beginning to settle in. He reached for the door handle but stopped short. He thought about the ditch. It was an awfully deep and oddly placed feature, especially when the road led to nothing more than a sea of matted vegetation. He wondered for a moment. Why was there a ditch all the way out here? What use would something like this be, all the way out in the middle of nowhere—"

Then, it hit him. His eyes widened and he felt an iciness creep up his spine before reaching into his chest and seizing his heart.

It's just like before. She knew we were coming. It's a trap, just another…

"Trap," he whispered to himself. He took the shotgun in hand and hunkered down in the truck. If the witch had laid this for them, she wouldn't be far, but another thought struck him. The witch couldn't have known where he was going, could she? But even if she had, even if she could see through the eyes of those demon birds somehow, it didn't make any sense. The rut didn't appear to be new, at least as far as he could tell. No, it may be a trap, but if so, it wasn't hers.

No. This trap had been dug long ago, by someone whose name was never really known. This one had been laid by someone that Satan himself avoided, the one Sam had set out to find.

It's hers. It's the bone lady's.

Sam's concentration was broken by a swift and abrupt scream into the night as crows descended onto the truck. There were more of them than ever this time, and they were pounding and beating against every surface, determined to please their evil master at any cost. They covered the vehicle, blocking every window. It was as if they wanted to smother him from the outside, make him feel isolated and alone.

"Fuck!" he screamed. "Fuck you *all*!"

As anger and desperation took hold, Sam drew his fist back and slammed it into the dash, releasing a loud scream.

Like a confused child does when a parent yells for the first time, the crows stopped dead in their actions. They stopped biting, stopped clawing and scratching at the truck.

His breath held, Sam watched with extreme focus as he waited for their next move. Surely, they were up to something. If shooting them didn't stop the onslaught before, there's no way in hell punching something would.

In one smooth motion, each individual bird lifted its head in sync, looking ahead of the wrecked vehicle, out into the forest. Sam moved his head trying to see what they saw, but there were too many of them blocking his line of sight.

"She's...here." Certain the witch had followed her wicked congregation to do her next victim, he held the shotgun close and checked the number of shells. Only two left. The first thought he had was to shoot Anthony, to make sure he was out of his misery, then turn the gun on himself and blow his own head off. She wouldn't be able to get him then, he thought. He may not get his son back that way, and he may burn in Hell for suicide, if such a place exists, but at least that goddamn satanic whore of a witch couldn't have *his* soul, too. He could deny her that small victory, by God.

Still frozen in place, the birds were locked on to something just ahead. Sam swallowed hard and readied himself for whatever might come his way next, be it the witch, or suicide. If the witch were here, he'd blow his brains out. That'd show her, he thought. If it wasn't her, he'd deal with it as it came.

13

Time seemed to stagnate as he waited for the birds to do something.

But nothing is what he got. They remained still, statues of miniature shiny black devils perched on every square inch of the truck. Sam stayed quiet, unsure of whether to be afraid or to rejoice for some strange reason. He moved about slowly, shifting positions as he tried to see, but nothing worked. Every time he thought he found a crack in their huddled masses, he looked into it to find more shiny, black feathers. Fed up, he raised his hand and slapped the windshield of the truck, an attempt to get the birds attention.

"Hey!" he yelled, hitting the dash and windshield repeatedly. "Hey!"

Nothing. Not even a flinch.

What the fuck is happening?

He reached for the handle and thought better of it again. The crows may be still now, but there were way too many of them to risk it, and Anthony couldn't help him this time if they did decide to attack.

They're fucking with me. They have to be. They were so hellbent on killing us, and now they're just playing mind games. Fucking goddamn birds.

He thought about rolling the window down and shooting, but that might be a bad idea. Only two shells, and thousands of crows. He might as well shoot himself like he'd thought before. He looked to Anthony, still motionless in the passenger floorboard. "Fuck! Fuck, fuck! What the fuck am I supposed to—"

He paused. Something started to happen. Something was wrong with one of the birds. Like a wave rippling away from a disturbance in a lake, the birds parted on the hood. In the cleared space, Sam watched intently as one bird collapsed to its side and began to convulse. The others steered clear, as if unsure what to make of their brother and his strange behavior. The bird began to writhe and kick wildly, its wings jerking open and closed in erratic fashion, contorting in unnatural ways. Its head turned around, exorcist style, making a full circle. Its mouth opened wide, cracking past what he could only assume to be the breaking point of its jaw.

Then it happened. Out of nowhere, the bird erupted into a ball of flames, thrashing about on the hood of the vehicle until all life fled its body.

Sam stared in awe, almost unwilling to believe what his eyes had just witnessed. "Wh-at the fuck?" he whispered.

In the corner of his vision, a figure that appeared even darker than the surrounding night stood out. A loud crash of thunder that shook the earth washed over him, and what he witnessed was like something straight out of a southern Baptist hellfire and brimstone sermon. Every single bird, each of the thousands carpeting everything in sight, burst into flames.

His back pressed against the seat, legs pushing hard on the floorboard, Sam watched as his attackers burned before him. He watched in both amazement and sympathy as the birds flopped against the ground trying to extinguish themselves. They may have been trying to kill him, but something about the death of a non-human animal has that impact on a person.

The flames from the thousands of incinerating crows cast a light into the darkness, splitting it in half. On the edge of the shadows, the figure Sam had noticed just before all the birds set fire moved. It was as far away as his eyes could see, and it was coming toward the truck, walking through the flames as though untouched by their scorching heat.

Sam gripped the shotgun tightly. All he could do was watch as the small, dark figure made its way closer to them. As it neared, he began to make out some of the features. It was smaller than he'd imagined at first, no more than five feet in height at most, he guessed, and based on the length of hair and overall appearance, it looked to be a woman. She wore what looked to be some sort of thick, rough textured black cloth, draped over a thin and frail frame. Partially bald, only a few thin strips of hair that were patchy in nature, fell over her eyes.

My God. I-it's...her.

The bone lady had a reputation in local folklore as someone who would punish those that dared trespass on sacred ground. This ground, Caldwell's Mountain, was such ground. Ground that had been cursed and left in the hands of the dead years ago. Ground that had been claimed by an ancient evil since before the dawn of time.

Sam hunkered down out of view, but as he did, the truck's front raised level and the door opened on its own. He jumped back and popped his head up to see where the woman was, but she was no longer there. "Holy shit," he whispered. "Where in God's name did she...go?"

"God can't help you here, Sam Fletcher. He's no different that you or anyone else for that matter. I don't allow Him on my land, you see? He has no business here."

Sam jerked his head to the opened door and saw her standing there. The bone lady.

"You brought those crows with you."

He opened his mouth to speak, but his throat seized. His mouth dry, he licked his lips like a crack addict, trying to coat them with precious moisture. "I-I didn't...I didn't mean to. I, uh, *we*, were trying to find..." He trailed off, his mind pulled in a million directions.

The bone lady smiled. Her teeth reminiscent of a shark's mouth, hundreds of sharp and pointed edges covering every inch of its inside, a horrid scent, that of rotten meat mixed with sulfur permeating into the air. "You're here to find some sort of answer, aren't you?"

"Th-the crows. They belonged to—"

"I know who they belonged to, Mr. Fletcher. I know very well whose they were. I keep track of those in possession of the dark powers."

"The...witch. The one from—"

"Gunrack Holler," she said, her voice crackling and raspy. She raised her arm to point in the general direction of Gunrack Hollow. "Mr. Fletcher, don't waste my time. I can assure you that I do not appreciate it when that happens. Tell me what you have to offer. Tell me what you want from me."

"M-my son, Danny. That witch took him two years ago. We were trying to...to get him back. We tried to get the book...the one with the symbol on the cover. I've heard that..." He thought about what he was going to say, finally realizing how ridiculous the whole thing sounded. But it was no more ridiculous that what had just happened. "We were gonna use it to get him back. But everything sort of fell apart."

"That book is not for your eyes. It holds secrets beyond anything that your kind could even dream of, Mr. Fletcher. It would do you no good, even if you did have it. Each one is different, unique to its holder. You've wasted your time with it, I'm afraid."

"Wait!" he shouted, not realizing he had done it.

"Yes?"

"I-I didn't know where else to come once she did this to Anthony. I've heard that, well that you can fix things. That you can…bring people…back."

"Two years is a long time. She took his soul away, best to let it rest now." She pointed to Anthony's body. "That one's not been gone for too long. I can still smell the life that he had to live. It was a rich one. I can give him back to you, in a matter of speaking. But the price ain't cheap."

He saw Anthony lying there in the floor of the truck. He'd given his life helping Sam chase down a witch that he'd never believed in until it was too late, and he wouldn't have gotten this far if not for his help. "I-I want them both back. I'll pay you whatever you want."

The bone lady laughed quietly. "Your daddy told you about me, didn't he, Sam Fletcher?"

Sam's eyes widened. "How did you—"

"He told you not to deal with me, yet, here you are. You know the price, I believe?" She lifted her head and for the first time her eyes were exposed. Large, coal black masses, shining in the remaining glow of the burning crows. "Your boy, Mr. Fletcher, his body's done gone *sour*.

Sour's no good. Not for bringin' back, I'm afraid. People who come back, even those that are fresh like your friend over there, they don't come back the same. Not like they were. Once the body's gone sour...well, they're nothin' like what you remember...what you *want*. Your boy's been rottin' away for a while, like all life does in the end." She chuckled and grinned. "Nearly all life, that is. Best to leave him alone. For his sake, *and* yours."

"B-but...the stories say that...that you can do it."

The bone lady cocked her head to the side, her smile fading.

"I'll give you whatever you want. Anything!"

"You don't have anything to give, Mr. Fletcher. You know my price. It ain't no secret. I require the bones and the flesh of *children*." She opened her mouth and a long tongue slid around the outer edges of her front row of teeth. "You don't have any children with you, from what I can tell." She looked past Sam and saw Anthony. "He'll make a decent trade, but his body isn't innocent. I only deal with innocence."

"But...I..."

"Go on outta here, Mr. Fletcher. Deal with your current problems before you end up makin' more for yourself."

Sam glanced to Anthony. "Wait!"

The bone lady stared at him, eyes squinted.

"I-I'll bring you the witch! The one who stole Danny's soul. The one who forced us to trespass on your land. Would that be good enough? She isn't innocent, b-but the souls she took...they are! They're not bones...but surely there's somethin' you can do with them?"

She watched Sam for a moment, considering his offer. "You will bring her here? You will bring the witch over on Gunrack here, to me? Why, you couldn't deal with her before, isn't that right? What makes you think you can get her all the way over here to me?"

"I-I can. *We* can!" He put his hand on Anthony's shoulder. "I'd need you to bring him back for me, though. I need his help. If you do that, we'll deliver that fucking witch to you right here, if that's what you want. She has hundreds of souls of, of innocent children…she told us so! You can have them all! Every last one but Danny. I want him back with me."

The bone lady chuckled, licked her lips. "That witch is one of the few of her kind left. Other than her, I know of only one. Lives in a holler over on Pine Mountain. Them witches, those like *her*, they have no place here. They're not natural, you see? They use pure souls to make a pact for their wicked ways. Her souls…" She paused for a moment as if thinking, then continued. "They are all innocent children, or of their parents. Only way I'll take innocent souls is for reasons of revenge, to right their wrongs. Do you understand? I work on barter, Mr. Fletcher. I don't kill for the sake of greed. Those souls need to be set free. I'll allow this deal, Sam Fletcher, but you'll need a bit of help. Those crows, they will do anything for her, and they will come in numbers higher than you could ever imagine. You'll never make it to her, and she knows that." She reached out her hand and grasped Sam's, extending his arm.

"Wait, what are you—"

With the index finger of her free hand, she used a jagged, claw-like fingernail to slice a long opening into his palm. "I need your blood." She rubbed her hand in his palm and smeared the blood onto her skin. She took a step back and plunged her hand inside her mouth and down into her esophagus.

Sam gasped in horror and jerked away from her.

The bone lady rooted around inside for a bit, then retracted her hand, handing something to Sam that looked like a sliver of rotted meat. "Bury this as soon as you cross back over the ridge. If you bury it here, it won't help you none. It won't be allowed from this land. But if you do as I say, it will protect you. I has to, now. It's now bound by your own blood."

"What...*is* it?"

"It's something that I use to make certain wrongs go back to as close to right as possible. Something that has no fears, no emotion. Something that she can't manipulate. It has an allegiance and duty to protect you and your family, Mr. Fletcher. Bury it outside of this cursed ground, and it will be there whenever you need it."

"But...what about—"

"One last thing, Sam Fletcher. This deal is very *unique*. One unlike any I've ever allowed. I have no sympathy for the likes of those who steal away the innocence of a child. their innocence provides me with life, and I respect that. It shouldn't be taken for no reason. You see, everything I do, I do to those who are deserving. I honor deals, Mr. Fletcher...pacts, to right wrongs. And I *will* honor this one, as will *you*. If you don't deliver that witch to me by sunrise, you or your soon to be undead friend will not like the outcome. Do you understand?"

Sam nodded, nervously.

The Bone Lady

The bone lady reached over Sam and placed her hand on Anthony's shoulder. "Just remember, he will not be the same. Don't let the outcome disturb you."

He began to stir, suddenly taking in a quick and deep breath. Slowly, he raised up and looked around. His eyes were glazed over and his movements appeared labored, almost as if his brain wasn't quite making the proper connections.

"S-S-SSSSSaaaaaaammmmm? Th-th-thhhaaaaatttttttt yyyyyyyyoooooouuuuuu?" He saw the bone lady standing next to them, and he smiled at her.

"I'm sorry, Anthony," Sam said. "I didn't know what else to do."

He pointed at the bone lady. "B-b-b-boooonnnnnneeeeee lllllaaaaaaadddddyyyyyy."

Sam looked to her, confused. "What's wrong with him? S-something's...something's wrong with him."

The bone lady chuckled. "Once they're gone, Sam Fletcher, they don't come back the same. I thought I explained that. You can't expect too much, especially from one that was weak like him."

"But, if he's like this, and he was only dead for a few minutes...will Danny be—"

Sam glanced to Anthony, then back to the bone lady, but she was gone.

No. Not Danny. H...he'll be different. He'll be... normal.

14

Sam did his best trying to explain to Anthony what had happened as they made their way back across the ridge, but his focus was primarily on burying that *thing* the bone lady had given to him. After that, they would make their way over to Gunrack Holler, and finally get what they'd set out for in the first place.

He couldn't help but be nervous now, though. Something wasn't right about Anthony, ever since the bone lady had brought him back. The entire time Sam talked to him, everything he'd said to him seemed to go in one ear and out the other. He just stared ahead, saying as little as possible, a blank expression on his face.

He's fine, Sam told himself. *He has to be. Hell, if I'd been through all that, I'd be acting weird, too.*

Anthony's head shifted slightly to the left, almost as if he wanted to look at Sam from the corner of his eye, but couldn't. Then his empty gaze went back to the road.

Sam wondered if Anthony could hear what he was thinking. Why not? Typically, that sort of thing was out of the question as far as he was concerned. Chalked up to craziness and phony psychic hotlines where African-American women talked in thick, lavish accents and claimed Jamaican heritage all for the sake of making a quick buck. But after everything that had just went down, nothing was out of the realm of possibility anymore. Sam saw the intersection ahead and slowed the truck, parking in the middle of the road a few feet down the right-hand fork.

"Well, this is where she said to bury it. You can… sit this one out if you want too, man. I got a feelin' you're gonna need your strength." He chuckled, trying to ease a growing sense of worry and tension between them. He waited for a response from Anthony, but nothing came. Instead, he sat in silence and watched his friend stare blankly out into the darkness. "I-I'll be right back."

He stepped out of the truck and walked over to the edge of the woods. *What the fuck is wrong with him? It's gotta be everything that happened.* He kicked a patch of leaves away and placed the thing from inside the bone lady's body next to him so that he could dig a small hole with his hands. *I guess she did say that he would be slightly off, but goddamn.* When he finished, he took the chunk of meat-like substance in his hands, staring at it briefly. "I hope this wo—"

A rustling shook in the trees above him.

He looked up and a single, solitary crow stared back down, its eyes glistening in the moonlight. Its wings outstretched, the bird let out a fast and sharp *caw*.

"Not again," Sam whispered. He clutched the black mass against his chest and, as he did, the bird plunged onto him, latching to his face like a parasite. He could feel the hardness of its beak searching for his eyes as it pecked at his forehead, every bite ripping small pieces of skin away. In an instant, he felt the pressure of additional birds against his legs, his arms, his chest. They'd been there the whole time, the ones who were outside the reach of the bone lady's wrath, watching him, waiting to pounce on him like a cat onto a wounded mouse. And that's exactly what he felt like…a wounded mouse caught in the savage claws of a thousand hungry panthers.

He tried kicking them, but there were too many. He rolled over and put his face against the ground to protect it, still clutching the bit of the witches' insides in his arms. "Anthony! Get the gun!" He yelled with everything he had as they ripped his clothes, bit into his limbs, but with his face in the dirt he feared his pleas were too muffled. He had to get up, to get out of there before they turned him into nothing more than a pile of bloodied bones for the coyotes to pick clean.

In one last attempt, Sam rolled to his back. The crows held tight, clenched to every side. He raised his legs high and brought them down, smashing them into the ground with every ounce of force he could muster. The sounds of the their bones cracking under his feet left him feeling accomplished, something he'd not experienced since this whole ordeal began. Immediately, though, more of the mindless birds rushed to take their place. He scooted back as best he could, finally getting his back against a tree, but their weight and strength was now more than he could handle.

They say that, before you die, your entire life flashes before your eyes. In this one particular moment in time, Sam would've attested to the truth in that statement. In the course of a millisecond, his life did, indeed, flash in front of him. He saw his father helping him celebrate his fifth birthday; his mother picking him up from his first day of school; his first dog, Woog, running around the house with a chew toy in his mouth. He saw a great expanse of water as he and his father fished at the lake, his best friend Anthony being—"

No, he thought. *Th-that's not right. What is this? That wasn't me. That never happened.*

In his mind, Anthony lay on a pile of old sheets in a dark room, his mother straddled on top of him, naked. In the corner, he saw a cloud of smoke rising into the air behind a camcorder.

He kicked a group of birds from his leg, slapped four from his chest with his forearm.

That's not right, i-it's not me. That's Anthony. That's...my God, what did they do to him?

The scene continued, his vision zooming in closer like a movie. The woman straddling Anthony turned to face him, and to his surprise, it wasn't Anthony's mother. It was the witch from Gunrack. She began to laugh, her tongue flicking in and out of her mouth and she grinded on top of the young boy.

"It's been a good ride, Sammy!" she screamed. "But, I've got you now!" She flung the top half of her body to the side revealing the boy she straddled.

Sam couldn't believe his eyes when he saw that the boy beneath the old witch was himself. She was in his head again, deep inside of his mind, giving him false memories to live as though they were his own.

"That's right, Sammy, boy! And to think, you thought you were hunting me. Ha!"

"No! No—"

Just as the wave of birds had fallen on him, Sam suddenly felt their weight being lifted. He could finally breath. There was a horrible sound coming from the road, a horrible, painful sound, like non-human screams of pain and torture. He opened his eyes to see Anthony standing in the middle of the road, the headlights from the truck cascading over him. The crows were divebombing him, ripping into his legs and neck with unmatched ferocity, but he wasn't even flinching.

Sam let out a deep breath when he realized what was going on. In each of Anthony's hands was a crow. His fists clenched white knuckle tight, blood dripped from the tips of each of the bird's feathers as if he were ringing water from a soaked washcloth. Blood coated his shirt as well, and it didn't take long for Sam to trace its path up and into his mouth.

"Anthony, wh…what the fuck? Y-you're…" Sam looked on as the birds ripped at every exposed piece of Anthony's flesh, mesmerized that his friend could take such punishment without giving in to them.

The same blank, dumb look covering his face, Anthony raised one of the birds to his mouth and took a bite from its body. Blood squirted, feathers fluttered to the ground below, the crow thrashed about as Anthony inhaled its innards like some kind of ravenous zombie sucking the insides from a human skull. Yet, the birds kept attacking.

"Anthony! They're going to kill you!" Sam pleaded. He jumped to his feet and plunged the black mass the witch had ripped from her body into the hole, quickly covering it over with dirt and leaves. He ran into the road to help his friend, but the time for help had come and gone.

First, they attacked his legs, then his arms, the reason fairly obvious to Sam. If he couldn't run or fight with his hands, he presented the birds with little trouble.

The worm, Sam thought. *Anthony was the goddamn fucking worm.*

He heard four loud 'pops', and Anthony's legs went limp. They had severed his Achilles tendons and his hamstrings, dug their beaks deep under flesh and tissue to

The Bone Lady

sever them with ease. Once his limbs had been rendered useless, a small group of the birds began to pick at his abdomen while another even smaller group plucked at his face, tearing his eyes from their sockets and eating them like cherries. Anthony lay on the ground under a blanket of crows, defenseless as they cleaned his body, ripping and chewing at him until his bones had been stripped clean.

Sam stood in shock, unable to turn away from the masterful cleaning work of the birds. Each time he tried, he found his muscles had stiffened. It wasn't until he vomited that his attention was torn away and he realized again where he was and what he needed to do. He wiped his mouth and made a move toward the truck, but the birds had heard his heaves, and they flocked to him like seagulls to a lone crab on a deserted beach.

There was no question, though. He had to make it to the truck. *Had* to. He'd taken too much damage now. His body couldn't afford much more, and the way the crows performed their almost ritualistic style surgery on Anthony's body in what Sam was sure would be some kind of record time – if times were kept on the speed at which a murder of crows can clean a human body – he knew that if they got him down again, there would be no getting back to his feet.

He ran hard, his heart pounding up into his throat. Adrenaline coursed through his blood vessels. He could see it! It was right there! The truck was no more than twenty feet away, but the crows were closer, and they were faster than him. He felt a surge of pain shoot up his left leg. One of the goddamn birds had managed to catch his calf with its claws and slice into his next to his Achilles tendon with one bite of its beak. Sam fell to the ground in agony, and in seconds, the birds were all over him again. He kicked at them, able to scoot backward toward the truck with his good leg. But they surrounded him on every other side, pinning him against the vehicle.

"Leave me alone!"

Sam heard his echo carry through the forest, yelling back at him over and over until it faded completely away. The crows, perched only inches away, looked at him with maddening hunger.

Why are they waiting? Why are they not atta—

His eyes wide open, Sam was all at once in another place. He could hear the birds in the leaf litter, feel them gripping his skin with their talons, but he couldn't see them anymore. All he could see was his father, Charles Fletcher. In his mind, he was walking through what he knew were woods, though he couldn't make out the exact location. He was carrying a shotgun, and he could hear others talking in the background, dogs yipping at fresh scent.

"Yeah, his cabin's over there, just 'cross the creek," he heard an unfamiliar voice say. "Some hikers said they saw something goin' on up here and he thought she might be usin' it to her devilish deeds. Sic 'em dogs on her! They can drag her out an' we'll hang 'er right over 'er."

He watched his father move ahead of the crowd, seeing through his eyes. His movements had purpose, they were intentional. He raised the shotgun and a small cabin came into view. "Alright, witch! Come on out here. We done know you took 'em kids, ain't no sense in makin' this any worse 'an it has to be. Besides, you ain't got no business doin' this devil worshipin' in my place or on my property."

Sam's vision began blurred and became shaky. He heard the dogs bark and growl, then cry in agony before their voices died down and disappeared.

A flash of light.

An explosion of sound.

Sam's vision went black, a faint whiff of gunpowder slid into his nostrils.

"D-Dad?" he called. "I-is that you?"

"You're too late, Sammy, boy."

He recognized the voice. A raspy hiss showing its signs of age.

"You'll make a good meal for winter, Mr. Fletcher. That's for certain. You're a good-sized boy."

Sam's senses heightened. He could hear the crows moving, but he couldn't tell in which direction. Away? Toward him? He wanted to let his father know that the witch was near, that the crows were close and that they wanted blood.

"Dad! I-it's her!" he screamed. The smell of gunpowder still lingered, as if the events were just now happening at this very minute, but he knew deep within his heart and mind that this was ancient history. He heard a cough, a gurgle, and his vision slowly began to give way. It was still blurry and wobbly, but he could make out a set of hazy figures; one on the ground, another standing above it. He closed his eyes and shook his head. When he opened his eyes, his vision had returned, clear and crisp. He saw that the figure on the floor was his father, the thing above him, the witch. She had one foot pressed against the chest of Charles Fletcher, keeping him down as he fought to be free. She lay one hand out in front of her and yelled a random slur of what Sam considered to be gibberish, then slid her foot up and onto Mr. Fletcher's throat.

In her hand she held Charles Fletcher's heart, still keeping perfect time.

"No!" Sam cried.

Leaves rustled again, but they were closer to him. The earth quivered beneath the figures.

Not the goddamn crows again?

The witch turned and walked up to Sam, placing her long, crooked nose to his. "I told you to leave me be, *Sammy*. But now it's too late." She put her fingers against his chest, her claws driving easily beneath his skin, sinking into his sternum. "Now, I'll take *your* heart just like I took your daddy's."

His chest began to burn in protest. "Th-this isn't *real*! You're trying to *trick* me!"

A bordering blackness that had crept into the edge of his vision suddenly faded away. The surroundings were familiar to Sam again. He sat on the edge of the road, his back against the truck, fully aware of everything that was happening.

The crows surrounded him, and to his front, the witch from Gunrack knelt, the claws of her right hand pushing deeper into his chest, just as he'd seen in the halucination. She'd taken his son from him. She'd stolen his father years before. She'd murdered his best friend and forced his wife to kill herself. And now she would take him, too. Rip his heart from his chest and keep him alive, just as she had done to his father. Dangling it in front of him like a carrot in front of a horse.

He fought hard against her power, unable to make progress. He felt his muscles contracting, pulling and pushing against some invisible force, but whatever it was, it was too strong.

He pressed his head back against the truck trying to create space, and behind the witch, past the sea of crows that carpeted the ground, the moon shined large and bright. It was full and beautiful, and all he could think of was how his life was about to end. Taken by the hands of the same witch that tore his family apart two years ago.

The ground shook again, a massive tremor. Leaves cracked and rustled close to him, but just out of his line of sight. *They're getting closer*. He saw them everywhere, the crows still like statues, watching him as if they were about to be fed a tasty human treat. And they were, truth be told.

Leaves rustled once more, louder still, closer. He couldn't take his focus off of the crows. He watched as they remained motionless. He looked at them, studying them carefully.

The ground shifted again, hard enough this time to make the birds stagger. They turned in circles, looking for the source of the disturbance. Leaves cracked and moved about on the earth, rattling and crunching under some unknown pressure.

The witch, still digging deep into Sam's chest as she tried to fetch his heart, began to twist her hand against his sternum. As her nails scraped against solid bone, the pain elicited from the trauma sent Sam into a state of something between pleasure and unbearable torture. The witch smiled at him. "Almost there, Sammy, boy!"

He opened his eyes for what he thought would be the last time. He was dizzy, his senses numbed. He was confused and everything in sight began to flicker on and off like a light bulb nearing its final stages of life. At first, he thought what he saw was something buried deep in the recesses of his subconscious. A false memory implanted from some childhood story or comic book. But as he bounced back into full consciousness, it only became more and more clear.

In the light of the moon behind the witch, a silhouette took form. The ground rumbled again, and Sam finally realized what had been causing it, along with the unexplained rustling of leaves he'd credited to the crows. At first, it appeared to be small, but it continued to grow in both height and width. Sam gasped, holding his breath as one large, bony hand emerged from the ground, followed immediately by another. They took hold of the earth, using it as a hold to pull something up from beneath.

Sam felt his chest begin to ache as his heart raced faster than he'd ever remembered. The thing in the ground let out a piercing cry into the night, and the image of the black mass the bone lady had pulled from her own body flashed in his mind.

It will be there whenever you need it. It has no emotion, no fear. It's something she can't manipulate.

Its hands planted firmly on the ground, the thing pushed its way up and into the world. The pain Sam had been feeling as the witch dug into his heart quickly vanished as he watched the thing emerge. Something evil rose from within, an ancient being, one older than time itself.

"Holy shit," he whispered. His eyes widened and his jaw dropped as he nodded toward the thing.

The smile on the witch's face fell as she turned to lay eyes on the great creature. Its waist narrowed, its arms long and thin, each finger ending in needle-like tips. On each side of its head, a thick and crooked horn rose toward the sky.

She huffed, terrified at the thing, ripping her claws from Sam's chest as it let out another roar that caused her crows to take flight, a roar that sent fear into her blackened soul. She looked down at Sam, her eyes empty and deep like bottomless pits leading straight into Hell. "It's tied to you?"

He pressed his hands against his chest and nodded.

"That means that you found...*Her*?"

"Th-the, bone lady."

The witch turned her back to Sam to face the monster. "Kill it!" she commanded her crows. "Kill it and bring me its *heart*!"

One by one, the crows descended like fighter jets diving in for the kill. They attacked it in waves, each one swiftly brought down with a single swipe of the monster's rigid arms. They went for its legs, perching on the hardened, black, tree-like flesh, biting and gnawing at will. The sounds of their beaks breaking as they tried to tear into the monster's skin sent gooseflesh up Sam's neck.

The creature moved forward, stomping, kicking, crushing small groups of birds in its hands like a teenage boy crushes a soda can to impress a girl. They continued to attack, but the monster was no match for them no matter how large their numbers. It flung them across ridges over half a mile away; squeezed them into black, feathery paste; crushed them under foot with each and every step.

"No," the witch said. "No! The boy was mine!" She pointed back at Sam who had now stood to his knees. "*He* is *mine*!"

Sam clenched his jaw tight to fight the pain from the puncture wounds, and lunged forward grasping the witch's legs, tackling her to the ground.

She looked at him, her eyes changing from obsidian darkness to glowing red embers in seconds. In a deep, drawn out voice, she said, "I'll kill you Sam Fletcher!" She raised her hand and clamped onto Sam's arm.

Sam winced at the immense pressure of her hold. Her grip was stronger than he'd imagined it should be. He reached up and took one of her gray, bony fingers in his palm, and peeled it back, twisting and yanking away.

She let out a scream that sent a shockwave across the forest with a force strong enough to break the treetops over.

Sam jerked hard and her finger ripped free from her hand.

She opened her mouth and her long tongue slid out toward him, extending the full length of her body until it wrapped around his wrist.

"What the fuck?" he yelled, fighting the pull of her demon tongue. He felt something behind him, pulling at his feet. He looked back to find that the witch's finger had turned into a snake, wrapping around and constricting his ankles. "Goddamn witch!"

She pulled at his arm with her tongue, the snake squeezing his legs until the bones were ready to collapse in on themselves. She had a look in her eyes, one of hate and hunger, abhorrence and pure evil.

His arm was only inches from her mouth now, inches from those sharp, yellow stained, rotting teeth. He saw the monster coming for them and he pulled as hard as he could, straining his muscles until they could give no more. "Not gonna be the goddamn worm!" he yelled, just as the monster clasped its fingers around the witch's head, ripping her tongue from her mouth.

The snake on Sam's ankles disintegrated into dirt, and Sam could breathe for a minute. The creature wouldn't harm him, he knew that. The bone lady had told him that it was his protector, and its job was to keep him from harm.

He crawled to his feet, his arms and legs trembling in shock. He stared at the beast for what seemed like hours but must've been only seconds. The witch kicked and flopped in its hands, cursing, begging for freedom. He staggered around for a minute, then got into the truck. He looked back at the creature, the witch still kicking in its hold, and he made the decision that now would be a good time to deliver his end of the bargain. He turned the ignition and headed back toward Caldwell's Mountain, the monster and the witch trailing close behind.

15

By the time Sam made it back to Caldwell's Mountain, the sun was just beginning to rise. He stopped short of the deep trench in the road, got out of the truck, and limped across to the other side. "I'm here!" he yelled. "I have your witch!" He turned to see the monster coming up behind him, the witch incapacitated in its powerful hand. "Where are you, bone lady?"

A black mist formed over a patch of bare earth in front of him, rising up like a dense fog deep in the mountains after a summer rain, slowly taking the form of a small, frail woman. "Voice, Mr. Fletcher. No need to be loud. It's quite rude."

Sam stood, beaten and bloodied, his clothes hanging from his aching body. "I have her," he said, pointing back at the monster. "I have your witch."

The bone lady grinned. "So, you do, Sam Fletcher. So, you do." She motioned for the beast to bring the witch over and lay her out on the ground.

"You can't just lay her down, she…she's dangerous. She'll kill us all!" Sam protested.

The bone lady chuckled. "Dangerous? You don't know the meaning of the word, *boy*."

The monster dropped the witch at the bone lady's feet. She cowered back, looking up at the bone lady with large, black eyes that showed a small hint of fear. "H-he was mine," she said defensively, pointing her bleeding stub at Sam. "He was supposed to be mine. I-I never meant to… to cross…*you*."

The Bone Lady

The bone lady crouched to one knee and looked at the witch, a warm smile on her face. "Of course, you didn't dear. No one ever wishes to cross me. But I'm afraid we have some business to tend to. Sam Fletcher belongs to no one but me or God, and that depends on my mood." She glared back at Sam. "It depends on how I see fit. You know this." She looked back to the witch. "He's honored his bargain with me, a bargain he himself devised, no less. As far as I'm concerned, he's God's problem, now."

"N-no," the witch said. "His family...they're, they're *mine*! Now so is he. It's my right! You can't deny me th—"

"Quiet, *witch*!" the bone lady said, holding her hand to her side and clenching her fist.

The witch's mouth slammed shut, biting down so hard that her teeth cracked.

"Keep your mouth *closed* when you are in *my* presence. Do *not* disrespect me again, or you'll end up as my servant, licking *your* blood from *my* bare feet as I dance in it. Do you understand?"

The witch ripped at her mouth, trying unsuccessfully to pry it open. She nodded her head.

"Good. Now, I said, the boy is free. As for you." The bone lady pushed to her feet and stood over the cowering witch. "Did you take his child? Young Danny Fletcher?"

The witch raised to her knees and attempted to stand.

The bone lady clenched her other fist tight and the witch's legs shattered into countless bloody pieces as if they were made of glass. She released a deep groan from her stomach, tried to scream, but the bone lady wouldn't allow her mouth to open.

"I did *not* tell you to move. Answer my questions. A simple nod yes or no will do. Is that understood?"

The witch nodded in agreement.

"Now answer me! Did you take his child?"

The witch fumbled on the ground, her legs gone from the knees down. She rolled to her stomach and started to crawl, using her arms to pull her forward. The first few pushes were strong. She was able to pull her body nearly three feet each time. On the fourth, however, her hand reached out and gripped something that wasn't soil. Something solid, hard as rock. No, hard as ice...ice, because whatever she'd grabbed was painfully cold.

Above her, a low growl made her body vibrate. Her hand on the unknown object, she tilted her head and looked up to find the great horned demon looking down at her, its body silhouetted against the bright shine of the morning sun.

She drew her hand back from the beast's cloven hoof and tried to scream, but her mouth was still clamped tight. She looked to its face. If she could look into its eyes, maybe...just maybe, she could get into its mind the same as she had Sam and Anthony's. Then, she could command it. She searched the outline of its head, but in the light of the sun saw only a blank, featureless void.

"Bring her back," the bone lady said to the demon.

The monster reached for the witch, seizing her waist like a child does a cloth baby doll. She screamed as its bony, claw-tipped fingers impaled her weak flesh, but the pain was only just beginning. The demon walked the witch back to the bone lady, tossing her down at her feet once more like discarded scraps.

"I know what you're thinking, dear. You're wondering, *why me*, aren't you?" The bone lady raised her hand and the witch lifted from the ground, hovering before her in the air. She reached out and took the witch's chin in her fingers, turning her head so their eyes met. "Typically, I don't hunt other witches. But you are an exception. You see, I know of only two of your kind that remain. The ones who *steal* the souls of the innocent. I have no use for such, weak and unimaginative...*things*."

She moved her hair away from her face and opened her eyes wide, showing their black cores. She opened her mouth, exposing row after row of sharply pointed teeth that seemed to extend down into her throat for as far as could be seen. "The innocent have a place outside of this life. You, on the other hand, belong with your keeper in Hell." With unmatched speed, the bone lady lunged forward and clamped her teeth over the witch's face. With each vicious bite, blood spurted into the air casting a scarlet mist over Sam and the demon. The witch's arms flailed for no more than a few seconds before the bone lady grinded her skull between her rows of teeth and reduced it to nothing more than a thick soupy concoction, like a thick milkshake.

Sam struggled with the deep and powerful crunches that came with the obliteration of bone, each loud snap causing his stomach to churn.

The bone lady continued, inhaling the witch like a python does a baby deer, feeding her into her mouth and down her throat with ease, her endless rows of teeth making quick work of any part of her that remained.

Sam stood and watched, speechless at the unbelievable act that had just taken place right in front of him. The swirling in his stomach grew worse, lurching up in violent heaves, and before he knew it, he was vomiting again. He fell to his knees, his face dripping sweat. His breathing was heavy, a mixture of shock and nerves setting in. "Wh-what...d-did...you just—"

The bone lady turned to him, her teeth and chin stained with the blood of the dead witch. Her long tongue flickered out, lapping up any remaining bits of solid material from the edges of her mouth. "Your son, Danny. Where is he?"

Propped on shaky limbs, Sam shook his head nervously. "He's...buried in th—"

"Get him. Bring him and *all* of the innocent souls to me. I will hold my end of the bargain, Sam Fletcher. You've shown your worth to me."

He felt uncomfortable staring at her, but he couldn't look away. Like the scene of a horrific accident on the Interstate when you pass it, no matter how badly you want to turn away, you just can't.

"Watch yourself, Mr. Fletcher. Remember, she *had* a keeper...the one with whom she made her ancient pact. He granted her power in exchange for the souls of the innocent. He will come to collect his debt. He will want them back, and he will take problem with anyone who stands in his way."

Sam nodded, acknowledging that he understood. "The one who walks in darkness," he muttered. "We heard the stories when we were kids. Dad always said he was the same as the devil."

"Something very similar to your version of him, yes." She gestured to the monster, who stood patiently, a dog waiting on his master's command. "Your protector will be near you until you are no more, or until I send him back into the earth. He will help you as best he can if her keeper shows his *rotted* face." She grimaced, her dislike obvious. "But know that he is very powerful, the only power in this world that rivals my own. Be careful, Mr. Fletcher, and go fetch me *my* souls."

Part IV:

The One Who Walks In Darkness

16

Acquiring the souls was the easy part. Everything that followed, however, was another story.

Gunrack Holler had been empty for as long as Sam could remember, the only path into it being an old logging road that had been abandoned before any logging was actually done. But the road leading to the creek that ran past the mouth of the holler was in pretty decent shape. He parked the truck at the end of the road, and from there he walked, following the crooked valley for no more than forty-five minutes. It was colder in Gunrack Holler than anywhere else he'd been in the past twenty-four hours, a strange sensation that gave him goosebumps. At the end of the holler, he found what he'd come for – a small one room block structure with vines creeping out of every crack, scaling the walls like hungry tentacles.

The place looked old, but not as abandoned as most stories had said. He tried to look in through the windows to assure himself that nobody was there waiting to pounce on him the moment he entered, but those that weren't overlain by the vines had a thick, white muck coating them. He rubbed at one of them with his hand, trying to clear a spot to see, but the glass was smooth to his touch. Whatever the muck was coated the inside.

Fuck it. I've got shit to do.

The door opened with no trouble. It wasn't locked, and it almost seemed to open for him once his hand fell on the knob. There was really nowhere to hide anything, the space was empty with the exception of one table, one chair, and a stack of old worn books in one of the corners. He thought about rummaging through them, looking for the black book of spells, but he didn't need that anymore. Besides, if what the bone lady said was true, and he had no reason to believe otherwise, that book would be no use to him anyway. He walked around back and discovered a crudely dug cellar, one with a door that had been covered with a year's worth of fallen and decayed leaves.

Inside, rows of rotting wooden shelves lined two of the long dirt walls, each of them filled with various types of mason jars and glass vials. On every container, a label had been placed with a name and date. The oldest he'd seen read – *M. Brosworth, 1731*. He tried to look through the glass to see the containers contents, but years of being untouched had caused layers of grime to accumulate on them.

Holy shit. She's been collecting souls for at least two-hundred eighty years, give or take. That's unreal.

He carefully began filling one of the duffel bags with the jars and vials, careful not to break or crack any of the aged and fragile glass. Once the first shelf was clear, he turned to the far wall and saw a group of small jars that looked newer than the rest. He took one and read the label.

B. Jenkins – 1991

"Holy shit," he whispered. "The little Jenkins girl from the newspaper."

He took down another. The label read: *T. Jude – 2001*.

"It was her the whole time. I-I was right. It was a witch. She's been taking children from around here for years."

He walked the length of the shelf, examining the jars at the front until he found one whose lid seemed to shine a bit brighter than the rest. One that had been collected within the past year or two. He held it in his hand and turned to the label.

D. Fletcher – 2017

Sam's eyes stretched open wide as he fought the urge to cry. He cradled the jar in both hands like one does a fresh, newborn infant child, and studied it carefully. Inside, a greenish-gray smoke swirled around, occasionally taking various odd and vague forms before swirling into randomness again. It was like the smoke was alive. He looked at some of the other jars, focusing on the ones with glass that hadn't yet stained, and each one contained the same type of smoke. Some were brighter than others, but each one moved on its own.

"D-Danny?" He said, holding the glass up to his face. He took a deep breath and exhaled a horrible, broken cry. "I-I can't believe it. Y-you're *here!*" He watched as the smoky contents moved about inside. He didn't want to set it down again. Why should he? Now that he had his Danny's soul back, why should he care about the rest of them? Because, he thought, they were the children of someone else who probably missed them just as much as he did Danny. Setting them free was the least he could do.

He set Danny's jar to the side and continued filling the bag. Once full, he rummaged around in the cabin for something else, an old potato sack, to hold the remaining souls. He placed every last one inside, except Danny's. That one, he cradled in his arm's, protecting it. He went back to the truck and, with the care of a new mother, he gently placed both bags in the passenger seat, buckling the seatbelt around them, then he put Danny's jar in the driver's seat. He stepped back and carefully closed the door. As he started to the other side, a familiar scent drifted into the air.

He stopped, sniffed it in, and he caught the memory of his father for a brief moment; the matches he'd used to light his pipe.

From behind, the leaves shifted quietly. It wasn't so much the sound of someone or something walking up on him that he heard; it was more the sound of a light breeze catching the dried, crisp Autumn foliage.

And he realized then, there was no breeze.

"Hello there, Samuel G. Fletcher. That is your name, isn't it?"

The voice surprised Sam, causing him to jumped back. "Where did you come fro—" He stopped mid-sentence as his eyes fell on the face of the man in front of him.

He was exceptionally tall, his clothes torn and ragged and looked as if they'd been washed in dirt. A smile stretched across his dried, cracked face, the skin of his cheeks ripped away to form a patchwork of holes exposing solid bone. Maggots writhed from the open wounds, chewing on the pieces of leathery tissue that remained. "I believe you have something that belongs to me, Mr. Fletcher."

The first thought Sam had was to protect Danny's soul. To take it and lock it in his arms and run. Run away as fast and as hard as his legs would go. But to run from this particular individual would be a mistake. If he wanted to save his boy, he would have to get him to the bone lady. "W…what do you mean?"

The man's arms rested behind his back, his posture unthreatening. He reached one hand out to Sam in a gesture of politeness. "Oh, I do apologize for my rudeness. Allow me to introduce myself. I am—"

Instinctively, Sam blurted the answer out. "The one who walks in darkness. I-I know who you are."

The man arched his back, a position that showed the full extent of his height. "Is that so? Intriguing. Tell me, Samuel, if I may call you that, how is it that you know me? I don't believe we've had the pleasure." His eyes shifted position back and forth between Sam and the truck as he studied the bags in the seat.

"No, we haven't. I-I've heard of you, though. I've heard the stories."

The man laughed. "Stories? Pray tell, young man, what sort of stories have you heard about little ol' *me*?" He bent over slightly, his face coming within inches of Sam's, and a large worm slithered from his right eye. Before Sam could react, the man's long, snake-like tongue curled around it, dragging it back into his mouth the way a child eats a spaghetti noodle. His eyes were a smoky gray color, a mist swirling inside like those in the jars. "They weren't bad stories, were they?" He took a step to the side and extended his neck to peek through the window into the truck. "What's that you have there, Mr. Fletcher?" He sniffed loudly, raising his upper lip each time. "I know those are my souls, Samuel. I can *smell* them." With blinding speed, the man's hand shot from his chest to Sam's neck, his thin, boney fingers clasped around his throat. "I can smell *her* on you, too, *boy*."

Sam's hands wrapped around the man's arm, pulling against the grip as he tried to free himself. "N-n-no," he choked. "Hhhhes-mn."

The man held Sam in the air, his feet kicking wildly as his throat was being squeezed into submission. "He was never yours, Sam. Blood relation is not my concern, nor is it my problem. My servant," he paused, taking time to look deep into Sam's fading eyes. "The *witch* you took from me, she collected *all* of these. For *me*. They are *all*, *mine*." His tongue flickered from between his teeth, its tip lightly grazing the skin of Sam's face, accumulating small droplets of sweat and dried blood. "Yesssssss. I can taste your fear, Samuel. Fear like that, well, it adds flavor to the meat. You will be most exquisite!" He opened his mouth bringing Sam nearer for the kill. "I will save your son's soul for my special collection, Mr. Fletcher. That was her intent, you know, to give him to me? I allowed her to eat those of lower quality…she needed something to keep her going for hundreds of years, after all. Danny, though…he is strong. Very high quality. He will be my personal lap dog."

A loud snap overhead tore the man away from his thought. He looked up to see what had caused the racket. Like they do when a gray squirrel uses the canopy as its own personal highway, the tree limbs were shaking above them. Something was there, running across and cutting through them like an angry gorilla in the morning sun. The man lowered Sam, slightly loosening his grip as he studied the pattern of movement above. He grinned. "You saw *her*," he whispered. "You made a pact with the bone lady, didn't you, Mr. Fletcher."

Sam struggled to breathe, wet gurgles slurped from his mouth as he clawed at the man's hand for precious oxygen.

"That thing is a guardian. What was your deal with her? Was it my witch? Or did you offer to bring me to her?"

Like an airplane crashing from the heavens, a large, black figure leaped down, landing next to the man and snatching him in its claws, causing him to drop Sam, whose lungs had never been happier as they inhaled deep and broken breaths. Both hands on the man, the monster squeezed and twisted him as if trying to ring him out like an old washcloth, but the one who walks in darkness was strong. He forced the creature's hand open, but it slammed him to the ground repeatedly before stepping on him like one does a pesky cockroach.

The man groaned in agony as he wiggled under the oversized demon's foot. He wrapped one hand around each end of the beast's hoof and pushed back against its strength enough to get his breath. He looked over at Sam, his gray eyes now an eerie, stomach churning olive color, his tongue whipping, teeth gnashing as saliva flung from his wicked mouth. "I'll kill you, Sam Fletcher! You can mark my words. You've crossed the wrong one, this time!"

The phrase struck Sam's body like a lightning bolt. He wasn't so much worried about his own safety, but he was concerned for Danny's soul. He watched as his demon protector worked to keep him from harm. It slung the man into a tree trunk, the snapping of bone echoing throughout the forest like a falling limb. The beast let out a cry and leaped toward the man, planting its foot firmly on top of him. It drew its head back and lashed out, it's dark mouth an empty abyss as it tried to bite into the head of the one who walks in darkness, but the man was too strong. He took the creature's jaw in one hand, the other he placed on its cheek. He began to pull, forcing them apart until a gush of black, oil-like liquid spurted from its face. It reared back and screamed, staggering only slightly.

Sam wanted to do something, but he wasn't sure what. He thought about yelling, but that was obviously a waste of energy, and there was no way he would stand a chance against the man's power superhuman. The demon slung its head back and forth like a dog that's been stung in the mouth by a bumble bee. It reached out and took the man in its grip again, but this time he was ready. As the creature's fingers closed around his body, he reached down and bit into the hardened skin. Unlike the beaks of the crows, the man was able to sink his teeth into solid material he began to rip and tear away at it until the thing's wrist had nearly been gnawed into.

Sam could tell that the creature was no match for the one who walks in darkness, and it was time for him to make his exit. He took the jar containing Danny's soul from the driver's seat as he jumped in the truck and placed it in the glove compartment. He had one more stop to make before going back to Caldwell's Mountain. He had to get to the cemetery. His only hope was that the monster could hold the man long enough for him to exhume his dead son's body.

17

It was nearly one-thirty in the afternoon when Sam drove his old pickup back across the ridge. This was the third, and hopefully final, time he'd set foot on the forbidden mountain in the past 12 hours. Digging the grave had gone well enough, the only exception being the combination of brute-like manual labor and the mid-day sun beating down on his already battered and tired body. But it was all going to be worth it soon. Every night he'd spent wishing he could have his Danny back, every tear shed over the loss of his only son, it would all be gone in a matter of minutes. But those sorts of minutes have a way of dragging on and on. They become the longest minutes of your life.

When he made it as far as the truck could go, he took the remains of his boy, along with both bags of jars, and lay them in the middle of the road on the other side of the rut. He collapsed next to them, his muscles giving in from exhaustion. What remained of his clothes, what the birds hadn't torn from him, were drenched in sweat and blood, his body covered in dirt. Various deep lashes and cuts adorned him; battle scars earned in a fight for the life of his boy.

"I-I'm here," he managed. "I…ha-ve…them." He dropped his head to the ground and closed his heavy eyes. When he opened them, the bone lady was there, standing over Danny's corpse.

"She did fine work. Can't take nothin' away from her for that." She took his mummified head in her arm and, with her free hand, lifted the jar containing his soul above her head, only to bring it down onto a rock, shattering it to pieces.

Sam reached out, clawing at them with slow moving fingers, unsure of why she was letting the soul go free. "Wh-wha-what's wrong with you? What are you doing?"

The green smoke it had contained began to swirl around in the air, zipping and darting back and forth like a housefly smelling a fresh shit. "You may be lucky, Mr. Fletcher. That witch preserved his body quite well. I'd imagined him to be rotted away into nothing by now." She leaned in and sniffed his body, making her way up to his face. Once over his mouth, the bone lady licked his desiccated cheek like a dog licks a bone. She smiled, the scrunched her nose scrunched and squinted her eyes together. "He's soured alright. No doubt in that. Not as bad as he could be. Still, flesh and bone that sour wouldn't taste right even if I *wanted* to eat it."

The green smoke zipped back and forth above the bone lady's head. She reached up and snatched it in her palm, much like a child does a firefly in a summer field. She watched it closely, her eyes taking on a strange look, one Sam would have confused for a look of longing or sadness if he didn't know any better. She closed her hand on it and looked up into the sky as she began to chant in a language that he didn't understand.

The sun that scorched his skin as he took his son from the ground quickly disappeared from sight. Heavy black clouds filled the sky and wind began to whip through he forest, the treetops swaying at its every command.

Sam watched, anxiety fighting fear for dominance within him as the bone lady chanted over Danny's body. He'd waited for this moment for years, ever since the witch had taken him away, and now it was happening.

Her arm disappeared into Danny's mouth, pushing its way down his throat up to her shoulder. She continued to chant, her words unfamiliar. A loud rumble of thunder shook the sky above and lightening dashed across the horizon in bright, electric waves. The bone lady removed her arm from Danny and placed him in the middle of the road.

"Boy just needs to be washed, now. Gotta get his skin back to normal, or as normal as it can be, I reckon."

Another clap of thunder, and rain began to pour from the heavens, flooding every pothole and filling every swale in sight with a fierce and angry current.

For a brief moment, all time stopped for Sam. As water pelted the earth from above, Danny's body began to soak it up, filling his dried skin with a new life. Every drop that fell on him was absorbed, rehydrating and allowing life an extraordinary second opportunity. Like something straight out of a science fiction story, Sam watched in absolute awe as his son – dead for better than two years, now – began to move.

Sam scrambled to his feet and ran to him, embracing him in his arms. He looked like Danny, just like he used to before the witch had taken him away. As Sam hugged him tight, he noticed that his body was icy cold. He didn't want to let go, though, and it really didn't bother him, anyway. So what if Danny was a little cold? Nothing a nice fire wouldn't fix. He had him now, and he would never let him go again.

"Danny, oh sweet Jesus, Danny you're…you're alive!" Sam cried. He cried tears of joy like he'd never done before. He pulled his head back to look at Danny's face, and he saw something moving beneath his skin. His smile began to wane. He placed his finger on Danny's face and he could feel something sliding. "Wha-what is this?"

The bone lady crouched down and placed her finger on his face. "It's a bug of some sort, I believe." Using her fingernail, she sliced a small slit into his face and pushed against the wiggling bump like a zit.

"What are you doing to him?"

She squeezed again, harder, and a shiny black beetle came sliding out of his face. "He's been dead for a long while, Mr. Fletcher. I can bring 'em back, but I can't make 'em alive, if that makes any sense. Only one can do that is God himself."

"What do you mean? He-he's alive now! Just, just look at him moving!"

The bone lady chuckled, a wry smile on her face. "He ain't alive. Do you feel him? Why, he's ice cold. He'll be like that from here on out, too. I can put his soul back in, get it goin, you see. I can make his brain respond enough to make it look as though he thinks, but his heart I can't get to. He's not dead, I suppose…but he definitely ain't alive."

"I-I don't care how he feels," Sam cried. "H-he's… *back*! He's *alive*!" He squeezed Danny tight, tighter than he'd ever held him when he was alive. "I love you, Danny! I-I love you more than anything else in the whole world!"

As Danny sat there, stiff and cold, his eyes fixed forward, Sam began to notice a strange odor. He tried to ignore it at first, but it only grew stronger with time. "What is that?" he finally asked, holding his nose to try and block it.

"That's your son, Mr. Fletcher. You didn't expect a body like that to not carry with it the odor of death, did you?"

"Y-you mean...he'll smell like that from now on, too?"

"I'm afraid so. You need oxygen to the tissue to make it live. I told you I couldn't touch his heart. As long as the blood remains stagnate inside of him, his body will continue to carry that smell with it. There's gonna be quite a bit for you to get used to, now."

Suddenly, Danny twisted his head and stuck his ear out, listening. He eyed the beetle the bone lady still held between her fingers, then reached over and snatched it from her hands, tossing it in his mouth.

"Danny!" Sam shouted in disbelief. "What are you doing?"

The bone lady shuffled to the bags and began to break the jars over the rain-soaked earth. "He's gonna have...problems from time to time. He'll eat things, do things that nobody will be able to understand. Eatin' bugs is the least of your worries, Mr. Fletcher. You'll have to keep a close eye on him, now. Closer than you can even imagine. Gotta make sure he don't eat somethin' else. You don't want him gettin a taste for blood, if you know what I mean, now do you?" As the souls escaped their tiny prisons, they elevated into the air, most of them going no more than fifteen or twenty feet before suddenly exploding with a bright green flash of light.

"Y-you mean, he'll eat *people*?"

She walked back to Sam and placed a hand on his shoulder. "He'll do better than most, I expect. They took him for a reason. He was a strong boy. His soul still is. But like I tried to tell you before, he ain't never gonna be like he was. His body, Mr. Fletcher, it was cursed by her when she took his soul away. He's sour, now. If he gets hold of someone, bites 'em, and draws blood, he ain't gonna be fit to stay 'round no more. He'll be like an old dog with rabies. Best to take him out back and blow his brains out with that shotgun of yours at that point."

"I-I could never do that to Danny!" he screamed, squeezing his son.

"Of course, you could, if it's the only choice you got. Most people don't understand that 'till they're forced to."

"No. H-he won't be like the others you've seen. My Danny…he's different."

"That's what they all say, Mr. Fletcher. I may be wrong, but I've seen 'em in all shapes and sizes." She put a hand on Danny's forehead and sighed. "I can feel it inside. His soul is strong. Seems to be fightin' for all its worth. That's a good sign. But you're gonna need to watch him closer than ever."

He turned to her, arms still tightly wrapped around his boy. "Y-yes," he said, choking on tears and snot. "I love him. He's my little Danny."

"Of course, he is. And he'll stay your *little* Danny for as long as he walks this earth."

"You…mean…"

"He's done growin', Mr. Fletcher. But you can't let that fool you. He's still gonna do what the sour ones always go and do. Don't forget that."

"That's fine. That's…perfectly fine." Sam's mind trailed off as it tried to process the information. "Danny won't be like them, you'll see. He'll be just fine."

"That's what they all say." She smiled at Sam. "Just don't make a mistake and turn your back on him."

18

Sam took Danny in his arms and held him like a parent holds their child. It'd been too long, and he had lost time to make up for. It was time to take him home. The thought was foreign to him now, taking his son home.

Home. Danny will be home. He smiled. "You're goin' home, Danny," he whispered. "You're gonna like it, buddy. It'll be just like old times. I even saved your favorite Berenstain Bears book for you."

As he made it to the rut in the road, Sam caught a glimpse of something moving in the road behind the truck. He paused, breath held as he squinted his eyes in fear of what may be coming. He was able to make out not a thing, but a person. Someone far in the distance was walking toward them. "Who is that?" he asked the bone lady. "I thought you said nobody ever comes up here."

She raised her head to investigate. "They don't. Nobody good does, anyway."

The sun was beginning to set, and as it slowly fell over the horizon, it lay perfectly behind the dark figure. Sam had played football in his high school days, and by all accounts, whoever it was had left the distance of a football field between them. It was a man, that he could tell, but the distance and the lighting made it impossible to gain additional information.

"He's coming for you, Mr. Fletcher. More specifically, he's coming for him."

"What? Who…who is that?"

The One Who Walks In Darkness

The man drew his arm back and hurled something into the air. Their eyes followed it immediately as it bounced on the ground, rolling up against the bone lady's bare foot.

She glanced at a coal black, tarry mass laying at her feet. "He's stronger than last time we met." The black mass at her feet began to thump, a thick and juicy substance pulsating from it with each beat. She picked it up and, without hesitation, began to eat it as if it were an apple. "The one who walks in darkness," she said aloud, staring at him on the other side of the truck. "He wants what that witch promised him."

Sam's eyes sprang open as what was happening hit him like a fully loaded semi. "Fuck. Was that the thing you told me to burry?"

She took another bite of it. "Yes, Mr. Fletcher. This is my demon's heart. It appears that he has eliminated him from this world."

She clenched her hand around it and plunged what remained into her mouth. She started chewing fiercely, the black substance drooling down her chin and dripping onto the ground. "I told you he'd come for you...for *him*." She glanced at Danny, then back to the man, but he was gone.

Sam looked around, nervously, inventorying every possible spot where the man could have gone to hide. "Where did he go? Is he on his way here?"

"He's not welcome here, Sam Fletcher, and he can't cross onto my land without clear permission to do so. But he will wait, Mr. Fletcher, especially for you."

"B-but...I-I can't go. I can't...he'll try to—"

"Take your boy into the woods, Mr. Fletcher. There will be an old cabin deep in the valley, there. It belonged to a dear friend of mine many, many years ago, the first in modern times to conjure me up."

"Pete Caldwell," Sam whispered. "It's all true."

"You will not be harmed there, and I'll allow you time to recover. But if you choose to remain here for any period longer than one night, there will be a price for my services, Mr. Fletcher, and it will be steep."

"B-but...if we go, then he'll—"

"That's right."

"But if we stay...what is the price?"

"In due time, Sam Fletcher. All in due time. You'll know when it comes time to deliver."

Sam looked at Danny. He was sleeping in his arms now, just like he used to do. There was no way he could leave the safety of the sacred ground, not with the one who walks in darkness waiting for him. But he remembered the stories about the bone lady. Everyone said that to deal with her was like dealing with the purest forms of evil. But right now, he really didn't have a choice. "I don't understand," he whispered. "What could you possibly want from me?" He lifted his head to look at the bone lady, but she was nowhere to be seen.

Sam glanced back to the truck one last time, and in the distance, a dark figure lurked in the fading light. A breeze blew across his face and a faint hint of matches filled his nostrils. He turned to the woods and walked in, down and over the first hill toward Caldwell's cabin.

END

About the Author

Tony Evans is a crafter of horror and dark fiction, father, wildlife biologist, and member of the Horror Writers Association. Originally from the Appalachian foothills of eastern Kentucky, Tony grew up listening to stories about mountain monsters and holler witches, and his love for these folktales shows in his writing. While he enjoys all types of horror, he definitely has a hard preference for stories about dark entities, demons, witches, and other monsters that may be hiding under the bed or lurking just outside your bedroom window. What's strange is that he claims not to believe in and of these things, though he is known to turn all the lights on at night when he has to get out of bed to go pee…especially after reading a well written story about demonic possession or ghosts.

His writing influences include Stephen King, Neil Gaiman (especially his short horror stories), Clive Barker, and Ray Bradbury. Tony has published over twenty short horror stories in various online and print anthologies to date, and his debut short story collection – *Better You Believe* – was released in February of 2019. He currently lives in Bardstown, Kentucky where he spends his time coming up with bad story ideas and trying to entertain his wife and two young daughters – his favorite little monsters.

For a look into his daily life and to stay updated on any and all of his fiction and horror related projects, follow Tony on Twitter/Instagram: @tonyevanshorror